Joanne Bentley had always l⸺ ⸻ furlough during the Covid19 pandemic gave her the perfect opportunity to revisit this lifelong ambition. The result is *Scarlotte's Memoirs,* her very first novel, which is based on some of her own daredevil and hilarious experiences. Like a very young Shirley Valentine, Joanne wanted to try out a new way of life on a beautiful Greek island – and like her heroine Scarlotte, she chose Kos.

Joanne currently works as a manager in the transport sector and lives with her mum Linda and her cat Purrkins. Her hobbies include drawing portraits of friends, keeping up with NASA (the National Aeronautics and Space Administration) and with science and psychology. And she loves eating good food – descriptions of which will always appear in her books! Joanne has travelled widely and also worked in the Middle East, but Greece will always hold a very special place in her heart.

*

Find out more about Joanne Bentley on Facebook:
@Scarlottesmemoirs
If you enjoyed this novel, make sure to read the next in the series:
Scarlotte's Memoirs
Back for More - Season 2 in Kos

Scarlotte's Memoirs

Joanne Bentley

ISBN: 9798682387281

This book is a work of fiction. Names, characters, places
and incidents
are either a product of the author's imagination or are used
fictitiously. Any resemblance to actual people living or
dead,
events or locales is entirely coincidental.

A CIP catalogue record for this book
is available from the British Library

Dedicated to Gary Jones.

You will forever be in our memories of Kardamena.

Rest in peace, my friend.

AEGEAN SEA

Lambi
Livadia
Tigaki
Marmari
Kos Psalidi
Planati
Mastichaki
Antimachia
Pyli
Agios Fokas
Emros Thermi
Piso Thermi
Loutra
Panagia
Valari
Limionas
Ellilika
Lagada
Kardamena
Kefalos
Panagia
Keri
Agios Mamas

MEDITERRANEAN SEA

KOS - GREECE

Prologue

A Saturday afternoon in May

Scarlotte Henson had braved her favourite polka-dot bikini today over the one-piece swimsuit she usually wore when going swimming at the local pool. She was lying on her sun-lounger, trying desperately to get comfortable and also to ignore the creaks every time she moved. She really should either lose weight or tighten those bolts because it sounded like she was sailing the high seas on the *Cutty Sark*.

Scarlotte was proud of her unusual name. Eve, her mum, had always loved the movie *Gone with the Wind*, especially the character of Scarlett O'Hara, played by Vivien Leigh. When she had her little baby girl, Eve had wanted to name her Scarlett but then changed it to be more original - and that was when she came up with Scarlotte.

Scarlotte was also proud of their garden with its lovely green lawn - which had to be mowed with stripes, of course, since she was a perfectionist. She would take her time going up and down the garden with the mower until the lines were perfect. Unless she tackled the lawn after wine o'clock, of course, when the lines tended to go all over the shop.

She breathed in the scent of her much-prized rose, *Rosa Aphrodite* – named after the Greek Goddess of Beauty - which she had purchased from The Chelsea Flower Show last year. It made her feel *very* upper class ('upper *claaarse*' as her friends would say). The borders were filled with ferns, flowers and grasses - one clump of which resembled a wild hairpiece that would not have looked out of place on either Donald Trump or Boris Johnson's heads.

Gazing up at the cloudless blue sky, she recalled the weather man predicting that temperatures would reach 22

1

degrees today, much higher than normal for May. 'Lovely weather for the time of year,' she said out loud in her best posh British accent. She was good at accents and liked to make her mother laugh with her impressions, not least her Russian meerkat voices from the television ads for the comparethemarket website. 'It's automated, Sergei. Compare zee market - simples!' was probably annoying her mum by now though, because Scarlotte said it every time any of the adverts appeared on the television.

A wasp was hovering around above her head, buzzing. She wondered if it was saying: 'Crikey, *she's* put on weight since I saw her last summer. Check out that muffin top hanging over her bikini bottoms - and what about those love handles, eh? Not to mention the double chin . . .'

Was it time for Weight Watchers again?

Despite having recently been treated for skin cancer, Scarlotte just could not help herself from gravitating towards the sunniest spot in the garden, although to protect herself she wore a wide-brimmed hat and ensured that she applied factor 50 in the traditional cricketers' white stripe on the nose fashion. She looked bloody gorgeous – *not*. Thank God the garden was not overlooked. The neighbours really didn't need to see that.

Scarlotte relaxed back on the sun-lounger, lowered her bikini top to get her front brown, and thought about all the years she had spent on this weird and wonderful planet. Where had those years gone? She would be forty-five (or forty if she was on a dating website) before you knew it.

Her mind flashed back to her past and some of the crazy things she had done. One in particular made her reflect how people could say something to you that would stick in your head for ever, and even influence the decisions that you made. For example, she remembered the time that she had been sitting in this same garden, much like today but with her mum's brother Uncle Pete - and how the words he spoke then had had a lasting effect on her: 'Bloody hell,

Scarlotte, your nose is *truly massive*!'

This one comment had really hit home. In fact, it had led to her booking herself in for a nose job at a hospital in London. She had received some redundancy money at the time, so why not splash out on some plastic surgery? She grimaced at the painful memory. After starving herself all night, she had been taken down to the London hospital at 6 a.m. in a private car by the son of the cosmetic surgery company's owner. The company had made all of the arrangements prior to the surgery, including the travel to and from London.

The long gravel driveway leading up to the hospital was lined with lush trees. A good start, she had thought, and her confidence rose. This place looked the business. However, her heart sank when the hospital itself came into view. It was like a crumbling castle fresh from the set of *Dracula*. Images of the surgeon wearing a black cape and having a mouthful of fangs dripping with blood sent a chill down her spine. God, what on earth had she done? Why the heck hadn't someone stopped her?

The reception area had old-fashioned floral curtains hung at the full-length windows and the dingy carpet was patterned and worn. The receptionist, a middle-aged lady with Hyacinth Bucket-style hair from *Keeping Up Appearances*, looked up and Scarlotte could see that her eyes were an icy blue; it felt like they were boring into her soul. Perhaps she had already been converted into a vampire by Dr Dracula.

After following said receptionist through a rabbit warren of narrow corridors and steep stairs, she was shown into her room. It contained a plain wooden wardrobe at one end, a single bed in the middle with crisp white sheets, and a small TV clamped to the wall. The receptionist quickly disappeared, leaving Scarlotte to 'relax' prior to her operation later that same morning.

The early start, the long car journey and anxious feelings

had tired the girl out. Yawning, she had a quick nosy around her room which had the same floral curtains as downstairs and a view overlooking the gravel driveway. Feeling the urge for a nervous wee, she slid open the door which led to the en-suite bathroom. Inside was a 1970s avocado-green toilet with matching sink. She saw that the carpet (how unhygienic) was faded and frayed at the edges, no doubt where previous patients had clawed their way out after having been bitten by Dracula. The whole place, from the inside anyway, resembled the interior of *Fawlty Towers*. Scarlotte lay down on the bed and tried to relax.

After an awfully long wait, Dracula himself made an appearance. He was in a white surgical gown, with rubber croc shoes on his feet and gold-rimmed spectacles on his nose. He had no bedside manner whatsoever. Definitely not one for small talk or pleasantries.

In his very French accent, which added to the drama, his first words were: 'So what are we doing for you on zees day, Scarlotte?'

Are you fucking kidding me? she thought. We had a two-hour consultation and now you are asking me what *we* are doing. It wasn't very reassuring.

After they had re-discussed the procedure, he disappeared. She was now starting to feel extremely anxious about the operation. Her surgery was booked in for eleven o'clock. Twelve noon passed, then one o'clock . . . and just after six o'clock, after Scarlotte had snoozed for most of the afternoon, as if by magic, a nurse suddenly appeared in the room.

Apparently, the surgeon was running a bit late, she informed Scarlotte. This was due to his previous patient having 'complications'. MARY, MOTHER OF JESUS! That was exactly *not* what Scarlotte wanted to hear. She began to cry, partly from fear and partly from hunger and thirst, and was still crying when the nurse returned to collect her for her operation at seven o'clock.

The nurse didn't speak much English and seemed oblivious to the fact that Scarlotte was sobbing and by this time, very distressed. The woman led her down to a small waiting area just outside the operating theatre where she was given a gown, asked a couple of questions and walked - *yes, walked* - into the theatre. Inside, five nurses were frantically prepping the area ready for Scarlotte's new nose. She didn't dare to look in case she saw blood.

Her nurse asked her to lie down and made attempts to stick the anaesthetic needle into her arm. At this point Scarlotte panicked, pushed the woman's hands away, jumped off the bed and ran out of the theatre and back upstairs to collect her things. Shaking like a leaf, she got the receptionist to order a taxi to St Pancras station where she stumbled onto an East Midlands train. Somehow, in a starving, dehydrated and traumatised state, by late that night, she had made her way back home and fell into her mother's arms.

*

The company who had arranged the surgery were located in her hometown of Nottingham. This was good because she would not have to travel far to ask for her money back. Lying on her sunbed all these years later, Scarlotte recalled how the receptionist at the company was not too sure whether a refund would be allowed, since Scarlotte had taken the decision at the last minute not to go ahead. Thankfully, Scarlotte was one step ahead and produced a number of photos she had sneakily taken with her mum's Polaroid camera: these clearly showed the grubby and dilapidated state of the hospital. A refund was duly provided.

Some weeks later, on a Friday night, Scarlotte bumped into the same receptionist in a cocktail bar in the city centre where she was sharing a few cocktails with her friends. The receptionist was a little tipsy and had decided that she was going to tell Scarlotte that she had had 'a lucky escape' from Dracula. Other patients had not been happy with their surgery, and she herself had recently left the company after being threatened with a gun by an angry patient who had also wanted a refund.

Thank heavens for Scarlotte's instincts on that fateful day. They had helped her avoid a bungled operation that could have resulted in a Michael Jackson-shaped nose - absolutely not the look she was hoping for.

But as the saying went, every cloud did have a silver lining. In this case, it meant that Scarlotte and Eve had decided to blow some of the 'nose-job' money on a holiday – a week on the sunkissed Greek island of Kos. And that was where it had all begun . . . Closing her eyes, she relaxed, let go and allowed her mind to revisit one of the best years of her life.

Chapter One

'Mum! Are you taking the suntan lotion in your case?'
Scarlotte was busily packing her large black suitcase and
needed maximum room for the compulsory seven pairs of
shoes for the week's holiday in Kos. Her luggage label read
We all have baggage and she had tied a red ribbon to the
handle which would allow her to pick out her case from all
the other black ones when it trundled round on the airport
carousel.

'Yes, if you like. Just leave it on the landing and I'll pack
it later,' said Eve Henson.

Eve was the most glamorous mum in the world. She had
a mane of thick, luscious blonde hair, beautiful bright blue
eyes, a figure to die for and, above all, a zest for life. Their
relationship was more like best friends than mother and
daughter, and they always had a lot of fun when they took
their annual holiday abroad together.

Their home was a three-bedroom semi-detached house
in a suburb of Nottingham. Scarlotte had lived there with
her mum and older brother Robin for ten years after her
parents had separated. She would always remember the day
when Robin went off to Brunel University in London to do
a degree in Media Studies; she had cried for the rest of the
day, inconsolable at losing her partner in crime.

The suburb wasn't a posh part of the city, but it wasn't
the roughest either. The estate had a mixture of residents,
from elderly couples to young first-time buyers. The
Hensons' house was stylish with a deep red leather three-
piece suite, cream carpet throughout and thick cotton cream
curtains which hung over the newly replaced double-glazed
windows. Eve's room was at the front of the house and had

7

a four-poster bed! Yes, a four-poster bed with silky draped curtains which could be seen from the street if you were nosy enough to stare up as you walked by. To be honest, that applied to most of the people round here.

There was a garden at the front and at the back, both kept immaculate by Eve, who taught her daughter how to mow in stripes. Scarlotte always found it amusing when her mum was out in the front garden, pruning the bushes or weeding. The local 'talent' would immediately start wandering up and down the pavement outside, trying to capture Eve's attention for a little chat. She definitely was the yummy mummy on the estate.

'Scarlotte, double-check you've got your passport and drachmas in your hand luggage!' shouted Eve from her bedroom.

'Yes, Mum, I've checked it fifty times now!'

Scarlotte was in the process of struggling to get her massive black suitcase down the narrow stairs without falling to her death. It was a good job that the airline had a generous baggage allowance of 25kg, otherwise she would have had to disappoint one or two pairs of shoes. She did not like to leave her shoes all alone in the house because they would obviously be incredibly sad and lonely.

Scarlotte was Nottingham's answer to Imelda Marcos. She loved buying shoes because shoes never made you feel fat even when you had put on a few pounds. Mind you, she was only a dress size 10, and being 5 feet 10 inches, she didn't need to worry about her weight.

Scarlotte now just needed to move her hard-top green (with yellow go-faster stripes) Suzuki Jeep onto next door's driveway for safekeeping whilst they were on holiday. She was dead proud of the sporty-looking car. The elderly couple Jim and Annie would take good care of her baby and no doubt on their return it would be looking clean and gleaming, having been washed and polished by dear old Jim during their absence.

The taxi arrived on time at five o'clock the next morning to take Scarlotte and Eve to the airport. As the taxi driver only lived across the street, there could be no excuse for punctuality issues. Eve would have been straight over there hammering on his door if he were a minute late. She hated lateness and was always ready fifteen minutes before any outing. Scarlotte had adopted this same attitude and would find herself tutting whilst sitting on the arm of the sofa by the front window, if she was waiting for a friend to pick her up at a certain time.

It was only a twenty-minute journey to the airport. They were lucky to have an international airport so close by, with no need for lengthy train or bus journeys to start their adventure. The taxi driver was paid his fee of fifteen pounds and Scarlotte and her mum lugged their suitcases into the Departures area. There wasn't a large queue at the check-in desk for their flight, because they had of course planned their arrival at the airport to be three hours prior to their boarding time.

After relieving themselves of their luggage at check-in, they braced themselves for going through security. Eve was often stopped and patted down by the security guard to check if she had anything concealed on her person. The only thing her mother ever had in her pocket, Scarlotte knew, was her trusty pink lipstick which went everywhere with her. It was pot luck as to whether you had a male or female security guard – but you could bet your bottom dollar that if it was a male officer then Mum would be in for a good frisking.

It was still only six in the morning by the time they had successfully completed the security process, so they walked through the duty-free shops towards the restaurant for a proper FEB – a Full English Breakfast. Before they got there, they sniffed and sprayed on themselves about twenty different perfumes in the duty-free shop; any person unlucky enough to be seated next to them on the plane was in for a migraine. Designer sunglasses were tried on and Scarlotte always sought out the most ridiculous-looking pair and posed with them on to make her mum laugh.

By the time they had polished off their Full English and had drunk a nice cup of tea, it was time to board the plane. Scarlotte enjoyed flying and was a bit of an aviation nerd. She loved the take-off and the landing but her favourite bit was when the cabin crew delivered their lunch in a foil tray. Both Eve and Scarlotte were in the minority of people who loved aeroplane food.

After the four-and-a-half-hour flight, the captain announced that they would begin their descent onto the island of Kos. Scarlotte and Eve looked at each other excitedly. Kos had a short runway compared to most, which meant that landing was even more thrilling, especially when the captain slammed on the reverse thrust to stop the plane from skidding off the far end of the runway and into the Aegean Sea. A round of applause erupted from the passengers as the aircraft came to a halt. Why did people do that? It made the girl cringe. She wondered if the cabin crew liked the applause or whether they also cringed at the jolly passengers clapping away like demented sealions about to be fed a fish supper.

You always knew when you'd finally arrived somewhere hot. The plane doors would open and you'd be immediately hit by the warmth of the air outside and the exotic local scent. Kos had its own distinctive floral smell which was intoxicating but would drive any hay-fever sufferer crazy.

Scarlotte took a deep breath of the perfumed air. They had arrived on the island for a holiday which, unbeknownst to her at that time, would bring two summers of the most amazing adventures and supply her with memories that would never, ever leave her.

But right now, all hot and sweaty, mother and daughter were taken by coach transfer to their apartment, which they'd been told was a short ten-minute walk to the nearest shops and bars in Kardamena. The apartment block, they saw, was only two storeys high and was painted in the traditional white and blue colours of the Greek flag.

The apartments were surrounded by many species of trees and abundant, brightly coloured shrubs. Plant pots lined the walkways filled with beautiful deep pink Bougainvillea flowers, and a path to the side led to lawned gardens with palm trees and more of the lovely flowers. The place looked just tickety-boo, Eve and Scarlotte agreed. Perfect for their week's escape from normal life.

The owner of their apartment was an elderly Greek gentleman. He was noticeably short and had white, neatly combed short hair and sparkly eyes. He wore light blue knee-length cotton shorts and a crisp white short-sleeved shirt.

'Kalispera, my guests, welcome, my friends. My name is George.' George didn't speak a great deal of English, but you could just tell that he was a kind and caring gentleman who really meant his warm welcome.

George helped them with their cases to the upper floor where they were given the keys to their apartment. The door to their room was an orangey-brown solid wooden affair with a gold round handle in the middle. The door opened onto a short hallway which led to their bedroom. The bathroom was on the right as you walked in and there was a large balcony door at the back. Scarlotte and Eve looked at each other and instinctively knew that the first thing they would have to do would be to check out the balcony.

'You go first, Mum.' Scarlotte stepped out of the way for Eve to take a look. After two minutes of wrestling with the lock which would open the patio door, Eve gave up and Scarlotte took over the task. Effortlessly, she flicked the button on the handle to release the sliding door. 'You really struggle with patio doors, don't you, Mum?' she said and grinned as she let Eve take the first steps outside.

The balcony had room enough for two white plastic chairs and a matching coffee table. Their view was of the gardens at the back of the apartments: it was more beautiful than they could have ever imagined. You could hear the crickets chirping away which added to the pure joy of the Greek holiday atmosphere.

Scarlotte and Eve were both really tired after their journey and it was now a bit too late to go out and explore, so they agreed that they would get some beauty sleep and unpack in the morning. It didn't take long for Eve to fall into the Land of Nod. Scarlotte knew this because her mother snored like a pneumatic drill. The girl always had her trusty pair of earplugs ready; they were a little uncomfortable, but they did dull the sound of the roadworks taking place in the single bed next to her.

Scarlotte looked at her mother and wondered how someone so beautiful and angelic could produce this God-awful racket. It wasn't long, however, before she joined her mum in the Land of Nod and had the most wonderful first night's sleep in the apartment that was to be their home for the next seven days.

Chapter Two

COCKADOODLEDOO!! COCKADOODLE DOO!! The alarm call came the next morning at six o'clock and would do so every morning thereafter. Although the noisy cockerel wasn't in their garden, it might as well have been sitting on their balcony, it was that loud.

Scarlotte opened her eyes to this new wonderful day on holiday. Eve was already awake and having a cigarette on the balcony.

'Would you like a cup of tea, Mum?"

'Oh yes please, that would be super,' Eve replied.

After making the tea and using up all of the little plastic containers of UHT milk, Scarlotte joined her mum on the sunny balcony. She'd dug out her fags from her hand luggage and lit up her first cigarette of the day. Cigarettes somehow tasted better in the warm sunshine of a holiday location.

They could not wait to put on their bikinis, cover-ups and flipflops and go and explore the area. Once showered and smelling a lot sweeter than they had after their journey, they left the apartment to seek out some breakfast. The road leading to the town was sandy and rough under their feet; it was quite manageable in flipflops but would be a total ankle-buster in heels. Scarlotte was already considering which of her shoes would be suitable enough for this terrain when they went out that evening.

It was eight o'clock and the cafés and restaurants were all busily preparing for their customers. They reached the town and headed in the direction of the beach. Both mother and daughter loved being by the sea; they had agreed that in a previous life, they must have been mermaids.

After walking through the main square which was lined with tourist shops, bars and people already eating alfresco, they reached the seafront.

'Oh, wow Mum, just look at the colour of the sea!' The water was a clear turquoise with tiny little waves lapping the beach edge. It was exactly as Scarlotte had seen it in the holiday brochure. 'I can't wait to dip my toes in it, can you?'

They smiled and linked arms then walked on in search of somewhere to eat where they could overlook this wonderful view.

A cute little traditional Greek restaurant called Angela's had wooden chairs and tables covered with thick cotton blue cloths. The menu outside displayed an array of traditional Greek breakfasts such as fruit and yoghurt with honey, various cheeses with olives and bread, and of course the traditional FEB. The choice was obvious. They were not strict with their healthy eating and a Full English would keep them going until lunchtime.

What they were not expecting though was for the breakfast to come with chips! Who had chips on their breakfast? They soon discovered that all dishes - breakfast, lunch and dinner - would include chips. Apparently, chips were what the English people ate with *everything!*

After scoffing their breakfast and enjoying the view they waddled off, stuffed to the brim, and headed to the beach. As Angela's was on the seafront, they merely had to go a short distance to reach the fine golden sand. The sunbeds were not occupied at this time of the morning which meant that they could have the pick of the best spot on the beach. Only two steps on the hot sand and you could walk straight into the sea. Simply perfect! They spent the day soaking up the sunshine, paddling in the sea in between kipping on the sun-loungers before heading home for a shower and to get ready for their first night out in Kardamena.

'What are you wearing tonight, Mum?' Scarlotte was just coming out of the shower and rubbing her long blonde hair with the crisp white towel provided by George.

'I think I'm going to wear my blue palazzo trousers and my white linen blouse,' replied Eve. 'What are you wearing?'

Scarlotte had of course been considering her outfit for the majority of the day, as she always did when she was on holiday. Should she wear jeans or her new knee-length khaki shorts? No, it would be jeans tonight because the sun had barely touched her white legs, which was more than could be said for her nose. She must remember to reapply the factor 15 more liberally on her nose as it was by far the nearest part of her body to the sun. Both Scarlotte and Eve used factor 15 for the first three days because it was considered then to be the most powerful protection from the rays of the sun. They would then move on to factor 4, which would allow them to tan their skin nicely before the end of the holiday.

The evening walk into town was not too treacherous in their flat sandals and they arrived in the main square without the need for the intervention of a Greek paramedic. Scarlotte had already been checking out the Greek gods who lived on this wonderful island and secretly thought that a gorgeous Greek medic attending to a sprained ankle would not be too much of a hardship.

Their resort had two main streets of restaurants and shops selling anything from blue and white traditional pottery to T-shirts bearing logos in Hellenic-style writing like *I love Kos* and *I've been to Greece*. They ventured in and out of the gift shops picking up ornaments of naked Greek gods with their members larger than their arms which made them giggle to each other. They would not buy anything on their first night, as they of course needed to go in every shop in the town before making their decision on which pieces of local tat they would purchase to remind them of their stay.

They eventually headed back towards the seafront to find a traditional restaurant that hopefully would have more on the menu than egg and chips for the British customer. As they turned off the street, Scarlotte noticed a little T-shirt shop on the corner. The shop looked cute and tidy and had what seemed like good quality T-shirts, brightly coloured scarves, bikinis and summer hats.

'Let's just pop in here, Mum, before we eat.' Something had drawn her to this shop; perhaps it was fate taking a hand. Once inside they browsed the lovely T-shirts and tried on some of the hats, being careful not to mess up their freshly sprayed hair. There was no one inside the shop, which was odd. Perhaps the shopkeeper had nipped off for a glass of ouzo and a slice of cucumber?

Just as they were about to leave the premises, the owner returned. On seeing him, Scarlotte stood mesmerised as if in a trance. Harps began to play. She wasn't religious by any streak of the imagination but at this moment in time, she could quite easily have been converted.

Manoli was his name and he had the most gorgeous big friendly eyes; his dark brown hair was stylishly cut with just a flick of hair flopping over his left eye. His face was perfectly tanned, and his square jaw belonged on a movie star. He wore tight, light blue jeans and a close-fitting white T-shirt which showed off his very toned body and broad shoulders.

Manoli and Scarlotte stared at each other for what seemed like a decade. Was this what people meant when they said, 'You will know when you have met The One?' Was this love at first sight? Scarlotte's heart pumped and she felt a blush starting to rise from her neck to her cheeks.

'Kalispera! Did you see something you like?' said Manoli in his exotic Greek accent. Not 'arf, thought Scarlotte - and she wasn't talking about his display of T-shirts. She had no interest in buying anything, however she would show Manoli that she appreciated his good taste in clothing.

'We were just browsing, thank you,' she said politely

and her mother nodded to back her up. 'You have some lovely things here. We have just arrived, so we are checking out the shops before we eat. We'll perhaps come and have another look tomorrow.' 'Perhaps'? she thought. 'Most definitely' would have been more appropriate.

When Scarlotte and Eve left the shop, the girl could not stop herself from glancing back and giving Manoli her best smile. He was looking right back at her and he waved. She blushed again. She and Eve raised their eyebrows and grinned at each other - something they did when they came across a particularly handsome chappie.

'Bloody hell, Mum, he was gorgeous, wasn't he!' Scarlotte sighed. She had a smile on her face like a Cheshire cat.

'Mmm, yes, he was very dishy,' Eve agreed. 'Now come on, let's get some dinner. I'm starving!' They'd had nothing since their belly-busting FEB.

They looked for a busy restaurant which was a sure sign that the food would be good. The one called 'Acropolis' was their choice as it was full to the brim with British tourists happily making their way through huge plates of fish or meat – along, of course, with chips. The two were seated at the only free table which was fortunately at the front of the alfresco dining area which meant that they could people-watch whilst eating their dinner.

Scarlotte chose 'dolmades' - stuffed vines leaves - for her starter and a swordfish steak for her main. Eve also ordered stuffed vine leaves but with steak for her main. Their food arrived quickly, and exactly as expected on large white oval plates with a generous portion of chips on the side. It was absolutely delicious, and with the help of a glass or two of local white wine, they felt full and happy, and a little tipsy.

Despite having dozed all day on the beach, the pair were still tired from their journey and from their working lives at home in Nottingham. Also, 'it was hard work doing nothing', as Eve would always say.

Scarlotte lay in bed that night thinking about the Greek god who owned what she thought was the best quality shop in Kardamena. Fantasies of Manoli sweeping her off her feet and riding off with her into the sunset kept her awake for some time before she finally dozed off. With luck, she thought sleepily, she would dream of him. She wondered whether he was thinking about her too - or was he that attentive with all of the girls who came into the shop? She hoped he was not one of those guys who flirted with a new female tourist every week.

*

The holiday was passing by far too quickly for their liking. A week wasn't really enough time to properly wind down and forget about work back at home. Scarlotte worked in an office in the city for the NAAFI (Navy, Army and Air Force Institute). The office was responsible for providing financial services, food and shopping for the armed forces. The girl liked her job but she wasn't particularly looking forward to going back there. Eve also worked in the city as an accounts examiner; she was far cleverer with numbers than Scarlotte's brain could ever cope with.

Each day in Kardamena they went for their usual FEB at Angela's restaurant and lazed on the beach until early evening. They tried out a couple of different restaurants but each time wished they had chosen Acropolis instead as the food there was far superior; the portions were also large, which satisfied their healthy appetites.

Ensuring that they walked past Manoli's shop each evening, Scarlotte would stop and have a little chat with the man of her dreams. He was such a gentleman and never over-stepped the mark of his affections, especially in front of Eve. This told Scarlotte that he was a good egg; he wasn't like some of the other letches who had tried to chat her up during their time on the island.

It was their penultimate night in Kardamena. Scarlotte had been flirting with Manoli whilst her mum browsed the neighbouring gift shops. She told him how she had fallen in love with Kos and wished that she could stay forever.

'Come back,' Manoli said immediately. 'You can stay with me and help me with my shop.'

Scarlotte's heart skipped a beat or two. Did Manoli really mean this - or was he just saying it to make her feel good? Doubts ran through her mind. Did he in fact say this to many other girls? How would she know if he meant it?

'Wow,' she sighed, 'wouldn't that be amazing! I'll tell you what, if you call me at eight p.m. on Sunday to tell me that you want me to come back, then I will.' She wrote down her home phone number and wrote underneath: *Call me at 8 p.m. on Sunday. Don't forget!*

Manoli gave Scarlotte his best wide smile with his pearly white, perfectly straight teeth, and promised faithfully that he would call her on the said day at 8 p.m.

Only time would tell.

They embraced and he kissed her on both cheeks. She would not see him on her last day as their flight was at lunchtime so they would be leaving for the airport at around ten o'clock in the morning. It was now a pure waiting game.

Chapter Three

Scarlotte had reluctantly got herself out of her bed and gone back to work at the NAAFI on Thursday which was the day after they had returned from the paradise island of Kos.

'Morning,' she said to her workmate Lisa. 'Did you miss me?'

'Wow, you look brown, Scarlotte! Are you sure you've not been rubbing coffee beans on your skin?' Good old Lisa would always be there to make her giggle when she had the blues. Lisa was her best buddy at work; she was tall like Scarlotte but had shiny brown hair which reached halfway down her back. Her eyes were deep blue set in her heart-shaped, beautiful face. Scarlotte always had hair envy when she saw Lisa and hoped that one day her own hair would be so lusciously thick. That was never going to happen though.

'Here - smell my skin. Not a trace of coffee.' Scarlotte leant over Lisa's desk and shoved her arm under her nose to take a whiff.

'Smells a bit like gravy browning to me, ducky.' Both cracked up laughing before Lisa stood up and reached over for a hug.

'Come on then, how many blokes did you shag?' Lisa took a swig of her coffee, waiting for the juicy gossip. Scarlotte could see the mischievous look in the eyes peering at her over the rim of her Notts Forest mug. Lisa was obviously dead keen to hear the best bits.

'I was with my mum!' Scarlotte objected. 'It wouldn't have been very appropriate to be getting off with blokes with my mum there, would it?'

Lisa never held back when talking about guys. The two of them would have many conversations about the talent in the office - or lack of talent to be more specific.

Sitting opposite Lisa at work was the only thing that

helped Scarlotte get through the doldrums of the boring work they had been assigned for her first day back. She couldn't really concentrate on her work with thoughts of Manoli constantly popping into her mind. She daydreamed about the two of them strolling along the beach hand-in-hand, with the glorious golden sun dipping slowly below the orange horizon. They would have just had a naked swim together in the warm waters of the Aegean Sea and had made love in a quiet cove out of the view of passing locals. They would get dressed quickly, giggling together at the naughtiness of their outdoor lovemaking. What were they wearing? Scarlotte pictured them in matching beige linen tailored shorts with T-shirts from his boutique. In her head, she had upgraded the little corner shop to a boutique as it sounded far more romantic. They would take this swim and walk every evening together before stopping off for a Greek supper of stuffed vine leaves and Greek salad.

A voice interrupted her blissful thoughts. 'I reckon you're not telling me everything, Scarlotte. You've hardly done any work today and you usually have a piece of cheese on toast *and* a bacon cob for breakfast. Yet today, you've only had one slice of toast. Come on - what's wrong with ya?' Lisa could always tell when her pal was hiding something.

'OK, OK - but you must promise me not to tell anyone.'

'I knew it! Come on then, spill the beans, you little minx.' Lisa sat up straight, all ears. As Scarlotte filled her in on the details of Manoli, the other girl's eyes opened wide and her jaw fell, almost touching the desk.

'Bloody hell!' she gasped. 'How could you keep that news all to yourself? That is so exciting! Do you think he will call you?'

'Shhh, I'm trying not to get my hopes up just in case he doesn't,' Scarlotte whispered as their boss Barbara frowned over her specs at them. They quickly got their heads down and got on with their work so as not to feel the wrath of

Barbara's tongue.

Every other guy whom Scarlotte had fancied at work suddenly disappeared into oblivion. Even William whom she had secretly adored for the past year suddenly did not seem 'all that'. He had nothing on the Greek god she had met on holiday.

She didn't tell anyone else about Manoli, in case he didn't phone her this Sunday. She'd look a right twat if that happened; in fact, she'd be the laughing stock of her office. So, she kept stumm and her little secret was kept between herself and her trustworthy friend Lisa. *'Please let him call, please let him call,'* she would chant to herself whilst lying wide awake in bed each night.

Thursday and Friday felt much longer than normal. The days at work dragged and it was frankly amazing that her battle-axe boss Barbara hadn't clocked her staring out of the window when she should have been checking delivery notes for the NAAFI shop. She definitely would not have been best pleased.

Barbara was feared in the office by most of the younger staff working there. She was a tall lady with grey, neatly tonged hair, held solidly in place with about a can of hairspray ensuring that not a single waft from the air conditioning would ruin her barnet. She wore oval-shaped glasses with a clear plastic rim, and when perched on the end of her nose (which was most of the time), they allowed her to observe her staff with a steely stare of disapproval.

Sometimes it felt like a prison camp in the office until lunchtime arrived and they all trotted off to the subsidised canteen and bar for a three-course lunch and half a lager. Yes, lager! The NAAFI bar was invaded by all staff at twelve noon. The men would enjoy a pint of lager or two for just one pound twenty pence, and then they would stumble off back to their desks for an afternoon of what was called 'the graveyard shift'. Scarlotte could never understand how the men (mostly the bigwigs) could down a couple of pints and still be productive. Perhaps they weren't and they too would spend the afternoon gazing out of their windows just like she did, although she couldn't imagine them daydreaming of shagging a Greek fella naked in the sea . . . However, each to their own.

The weekend finally arrived. Scarlotte had popped into town on the number 28 bus to Snappy Snaps, to get her holiday photos developed. Snappy Snaps were the best in town. If you paid a bit extra, the photos could be ready for collection in an hour. There was nothing more exciting than taking your film to be developed. Digital cameras were only just being released and were way out of Scarlotte's budget. With her old-fashioned camera you just had to point, click - and hope that your fat finger was not in front of the lens and hence buggering up your snaps. Snappy Snaps would apply stickers to the crap photos to tell you where you had gone wrong with your amateur photography skills. Scarlotte was sure they had run out of stickers after processing her last batch of photos from Christmas Day.

'What size photos would you like?' The young male shop assistant lacked her own enthusiasm for her photo developing. He wore a baggy black T-shirt with jeans and his messy brown hair looked like he had literally just got out of bed. He had a very bored expression on his face and was very obviously not in the mood for work today. She could sympathise with that!

'The largest photos, please. How long will it take?' It was going to be just over an hour because they were busy today. The time would have to be filled by buying more things that she *needed* in the clothes shop. What a chore, she giggled to herself.

After one hour exactly, Scarlotte returned to the Snappy Snaps shop to collect her photos. Of course, the only pix she would be interested in were the ones taken by Mum of herself and Manoli. Please let them turn out OK, she thought. If Manoli did call her tomorrow, she would need some good shots of her new love to show to Lisa.

The same bored shop assistant asked for the fee of £3.99 for the twenty-eight photos - a small price to pay for an envelope of precious memories. Scarlotte paid and waited with bated breath for her envelope to be identified from the rows of developed photos behind the counter. Once the package was in her hand she rushed to the exit and stood outside, where she carefully tore open the sealed yellow envelope which contained the wallet of photos. No way would she be able to wait until she got on the bus to look at them. This was one of those times when patience definitely did not need to be a virtue.

Extra-cautious not to put her fingerprints on the front of them, she removed the photos from their crisp envelope. What would the first photo be? Would it be of Manoli's wide, mesmerising smile? Well, no, it would not. The first shot was of the apartments. . . *Boring,* she thought. Why did we take photos of things that wouldn't be that interesting afterwards? Everyone knows that the best photos have real, live, actual human beings in them.

She flicked through photos taken of plates of food, of the beach, the blue and white buildings - and the many lovely shots of her and her mum raising their glasses to the unsuspecting photographer who had been terrorised into taking their picture. Finally, right near the back of the pile there he was, the Greek god himself - Manoli - with his arms wrapped around Scarlotte's waist. She felt her face flush and her heart flutter as a massive smile appeared on her lips. Passers-by would probably think that she had a screw loose and that she was experiencing some sort of fit.

In the photo she was wearing her leather trousers made in the fashionable peg style and a black strappy crop-top. Her eyes shone at the camera lens with great happiness and her blonde hair fell over her left shoulder. Manoli wore his light blue baggy jeans and his white fitted T-shirt. His hair was freshly washed and flopped over his eyes which were like chocolate Minstrels - she would like to lick them to see if they tasted just as delicious as they looked. He was gazing at the camera with a huge smile and what she would describe as love.

Was it love? Scarlotte asked herself. Well, she would just have to wait until tomorrow to find out if his affections were real. She could not wait now to get on that number 28 double-decker bus to ride home to Eve and show her the fab photos.

*

'Mmmm, dinner smells amazing, Mum.' Eve was cooking a proper dinner of roast beef, roast potatoes and veg with lashings of gravy. In their house, they liked to eat their weekend dinner at teatime. Delicious smells wafted around the air and made Scarlotte's mouth water.

'Roast beef and Yorkshire pudding, your favourite today!' Eve called from the steamy kitchen. 'Did you get the photos?'

'Yes, Mum, and they're great. Want to look at them now?'

'Let's have our dinner and then we can relax on the sofa and look at them together. Did the ones of you and Manoli turn out all right?' Eve was not the best photographer and would often be the reason for Snappy Snaps applying their 'could have done better' stickers on the photos.

The dinner was as delicious as anticipated. Scarlotte usually wolfed it down in a couple of minutes. Tonight, though, she struggled to eat it all as she was excited but also anxious for tomorrow when the clock would turn to eight o'clock. She would know when the time had arrived as the theme tune to the ending of *The Antiques Roadshow* would be blasting out of the telly.

'Ah, that's a nice one . . . that's a good one . . . oooh, that's a lovely one of you and me,' Eve would say about every photo. They spent a good hour looking at the pictures and reminiscing about the good times that they had had.

Sunday was a day of rest and both Scarlotte and her mum had a little lie-in. Then Scarlotte spent the day sorting out her wardrobe and adding clothes she didn't want to a charity bag, whilst Eve did the week's ironing in front of the television.

They had beef sandwiches for tea made from yesterday's leftover meat. Eve would always put lashing of butter on the white bread which was just delicious. They sat watching TV as they ate their sandwiches with a lovely cuppa tea.

At eight o'clock and exactly on cue, the end theme tune to *The Antiques Roadshow* started to play after one lucky person had been told that the painting which they had found in their loft was worth a hefty £20,000. They would not be selling the painting, of course, because it was now apparently 'a family heirloom'.

'Yeah right, of course you won't be selling it,' scoffed Scarlotte.

'I'd be straight down the auction the next morning,' said Eve, laughing. She would have too!

Then there was silence . . . for what felt like an eternity. Scarlotte looked at Eve with sad, glistening eyes as the phone didn't ring.

'He'll call, my love, I just know he will. And if he doesn't – well, it's his bloody loss, isn't it.' Eve gave her daughter her words of support.

Scarlotte's heart was slowly sinking further and further down into her chest. Manoli was not going to call, and all her hopes for a new life in Kos sadly tumbled into oblivion. Then at three minutes past eight, from the hallway they heard it! *Ring ring, ring ring, ring ring . . .* The piercing sound broke the silence and the tension.

Chapter Four

'I don't want it that much,' snorted the fat arrogant owner of the jeep garage which was around the corner from their house. Scarlotte imagined him sitting behind his large desk, with the head of a pig on top of his body, a fat cigar held in his trotters and shouting orders at his piglets.

Scarlotte was trying to get herself a tidy profit on her much-loved racing green Suzuki Santana. Her mum had helped her to buy it before her driving test, which she'd passed first time. The insurance was expensive for a new driver as young as her but she loved that car; it was so cool with its yellow go-faster stripes down the side. Even the cat had enjoyed going for a spin in the back. Joshy was a brown Persian with long silky hair which Scarlotte brushed every day. His eyes were the brightest orange and they would look at you with longing eyes begging for cuddles. The girl knew that her mum would look after him whilst she was away, but she would miss her fur baby dearly.

Scarlotte left the garage feeling quite shaken by the unpleasant treatment from Mr Porker. She instantly called her dad. Roger Henson didn't live with them any more since he and Eve had divorced ten years earlier, but he was always there for his kids. And if Scarlotte needed help with a car, her dad was always her first port of call.

'He said *what* to you?' her dad exclaimed at the other end of the phone. 'I'll bloody go to his garage and pour brake fluid on his cars! That guy needs teaching a lesson, bigtime.'

Roger would not stand for anyone upsetting his daughter and although he was only joking, Scarlotte knew that he would 'send the boys round' if she wanted him to. She giggled to herself at the thought of her balaclava-clad dad sneaking to the jeep garage under cover of night armed with a rusty can of the fluid.

'Don't worry, love, we'll get it sorted for you. If you can't sell it before you leave in two weeks' time, I'll sell it for you. How about that?'

'Thanks, Dad. I'll try advertising it in the local paper this week and hopefully someone will fall in love with it.'

A week later on Saturday morning a young lad purchasing his first car kindly took the jeep off her hands. 'Would you accept £2800?' The price was £3000 but Scarlotte really needed the money.

'How about £2900 and you've got a deal?' she suggested with her biggest cheeky grin which most young guys could not resist.

He had agreed and she waved goodbye to her funky jeep with a tear in her eye. Their time together had been short but very sweet. However, she now had £2900 in her hand which meant that she could book a flight to Kos and some accommodation for the following week.

'Thank God for that, Mum. Do you fancy coming into town with me so I can book my flight?' she asked. Eve was cleaning the house in her dressing-gown, but agreed immediately. First, of course, she would need to shower, do her hair and put on her make-up - and then they would be off to the travel agents.

Scarlotte had handed in her notice on the Monday after telling Lisa first, of course, and then the rest of her work colleagues her plans. With her glasses perched on the end of her nose, the boss Barbara had taken the letter of resignation from her but not opened it immediately. As usual when anyone went to ask her something, she made Scarlotte wait at her desk before finally looking up with that expression which meant 'I am very busy and important, and you are disturbing me with your silly little matters.'

Barbara finally opened the crisp white and smartly written envelope. 'Oh! So you're leaving us. I wish *I* could go swanning off to Greece for the summer,' was her only reaction. Barbara did not like any of her minions doing anything even slightly more exciting than herself.

This response gave Scarlotte great satisfaction, since Barbara's jealousy was almost tangible. She was dismissed like a naughty schoolchild and scuttled off back to her own desk with a huge grin on her face. Lisa caught her eye as she returned to her seat and she gave Scarlotte a massive great wink.

*

A return flight and accommodation were booked for the coming Saturday to the island of Kos. Scarlotte would stay in an apartment for the first week as she did not wish to move straight in with Manoli without checking out his digs first. What if his place was a dive? What if it was dirty? What would she do? The return ticket was insurance: if she found that she had made a mistake, or she didn't like it there, she would have the security of a ticket back to the UK a week later. Scarlotte really hoped that the return flight would not be necessary, so the plane could leave with her seat vacant, giving the lucky person next to it the luxury of more elbow room.

Whilst in town on the Saturday, she had purchased a new backpacker's rucksack which was so 'cool' and would be easier to carry around than her massive black suitcase. She had wondered whether she was allowed to buy a rucksack, as she was not a student on a gap year, she wasn't island hopping or travelling through Thailand or Vietnam. She definitely was not any of those things, but at least she would look like a proper traveller with the large grey and blue clothes-carrying device proudly displayed on her back

Scarlotte's last week at work had been really dull. She did hardly any work but spent most of her time wandering around the five floors of offices chatting with colleagues to tell them that she was leaving, much to Barbara's disapproval. When Friday finally arrived, she left the office feeling a little bit sad but armed with flowers from her friends there and a beach towel from Lisa. She and Scarlotte promised to stay in touch as much as possible. They would speak from phone boxes and write letters to each other that would no doubt take weeks to arrive.

'Have a great time, Minxy, and make sure you write to let me know what's going on.' Lisa wrapped her arms around Scarlotte and gave her a huge hug and a smacker of a kiss on her cheek. With glistening eyes, Scarlotte walked down the hill from the NAAFI to her bus stop, turning to wave goodbye to Lisa. She would miss her mate with her dry but silly sense of humour.

Eve had secretly invited the family over on Friday night for a buffet of cheese and onion sandwiches, crisps, quiche and trifle. Eve knew that sherry trifle was Scarlotte's favourite.

The front room was decorated with blue and white balloons to symbolise the Greek flag. The large solid wood table had been extended to its full length to accommodate the mass of culinary delights. Uncles, aunts and friends had arrived and found themselves a comfy spot on the sofa or chairs ready to start the feast.

'*Surprise!*' shouted Eve as Scarlotte struggled through the front door with her gifts from work. Everyone stood up ready to welcome her to the party. Big smiles and hugs awaited her in the front room and the buffet on the table looked lip-smackingly delicious.

'Oh my God, Mum!' Scarlotte dropped her presents on the porch floor and entered the lounge feeling overwhelmed. She gulped back the tears and gave everyone a massive cuddle. She was not a fan of farewells and already knew that this evening would end with her sobbing into her mum's shoulder.

The party was lovely, the food duly scoffed up, and after a couple of hours the family said their well-wishes and left, leaving Eve and Scarlotte to polish off the last bit of trifle. To her surprise, Scarlotte didn't get emotional as she had anticipated, and she felt all warm and fuzzy inside from the many kind words of encouragement for her new life in Greece.

After clearing the table of the leftovers and covering the last few sandwiches with clingfilm to keep them fresh for tomorrow, Scarlotte and Eve trotted off to bed feeling weary from the day's excitement. Scarlotte set her alarm for eight o'clock in the morning to give herself enough time to finish cramming her new purchases into her rucksack. She knew that she would find it hard to nod off that night as she was so excited about tomorrow.

'Have you got your passport, tickets and drachmas?' Eve shouted to Scarlotte as she trundled precariously down the stairs – but this time with her rucksack instead of the massive black suitcase.

'Yes, Mum, I have checked twenty times.' And this time she really had checked twenty times. Can you imagine getting to the airport, just about to say your goodbyes only to discover that you'd stupidly left your passport on your dressing-table? Were people really that careless? Why didn't they do what she and her mum did and check the compulsory twenty to fifty times before leaving their homes?

Scarlotte had impressed herself by managing to squeeze every item of clothing and footwear into her rucksack. It was literally bursting at the seams and she had fears of her knickers making their way out of the seams and proudly displaying themselves on the carousel at the other end. Good job they were all new knickers, she thought - dirty knickers on the carousel would have been hideously embarrassing. She hadn't packed any heeled shoes this time because the stilettos would surely puncture the material and make everything fall out into the hold of the airplane.

Eve and her brother, Scarlotte's Uncle Pete took Scarlotte to the airport and she was greeted there by two friends from the NAAFI. The sight of them made her burst into tears.

'What the bloody hell are you doing here?' she shouted as

she ran towards them for a massive three-way cuddle.

'Hahaha - surprise! Did you think we could let you leave without making sure you'd actually buggered off on that plane,' said Lisa.

Lisa was guaranteed to make Scarlotte laugh at the saddest of times. They would often be caught by Barbara at work for giggling, as Scarlotte's shoulders shaking up and down would give them away. She thought about the times when she and Lisa would listen on their headphones to Steve Wright on Radio One and crack up laughing at his silly humour. Scarlotte loved that Karen and Lisa were there along with her mum and uncle to see her off as she felt excited but also nervous about her new adventure. It was different, going to Kos all on her own.

Scarlotte checked in her rucksack at the airline desk and waited in anticipation for the scales to tell her that her luggage was overweight. This would of course result in her rummaging around her rucksack and having to remove certain items of clothing or shoes and give them to her mum to take home. It would be an impossible task as she absolutely 'needed' every single item. A bit like when you go shopping for shoes and there is always one pair that you feel your life cannot continue without.

The check-in desk lady was a very pretty brunette. Her hair tied neatly in a bun and her perfectly applied make-up and red lipstick all contributed to the air hostess look. 'That's all fine,' she said, smiling. 'Here's your boarding pass and you can now proceed to security.'

Scarlotte released her held breath as she was starting to turn a deep shade of red and smiled widely back at the check-in lady.

It was now time for the horrible part of her journey which was to say her goodbyes to her mum, uncle and friends. Scarlotte really loved life and always looked for the positive in any situation but she simply could not handle having to say goodbye. She would have found it so much easier to have said her farewells at home and gone to the airport on her own. But now she had no choice but to go through the heart-wrenching task.

Lisa and Karen gave Scarlotte another massive cuddle, telling her to keep in touch, which she would of course. Then her uncle embraced her and finally her mum. Scarlotte began to cry as she gave Eve the most massive bear hug.

'Don't cry because you'll make me cry!' Eve always said this if Scarlotte was crying and it was true; if either of them cried then the other would start blubbering too. 'You're going to have a great time. Ring me as soon as you get there, won't you.'

'I will, Mum, and I'll call you as often as I can.' Saying this made Scarlotte and Eve both feel a little better about her departure. Scarlotte found it easier to tell herself that she was merely going on holiday for a couple of weeks and that she would be back soon. This would help her through.

Scarlotte turned around and gave a final wave as she entered security. She could see that Eve was smiling broadly and she thought, I bet Mum will enjoy having the house to herself. She'll be having parties and playing her music loud, annoying the neighbours. She knew this wasn't true though and they would both miss each other dearly.

*

Scarlotte was seated in row 33A which meant she had a window seat. She always booked a window seat because although she was terrified of heights, she loved to look out and see the fluffy white clouds beneath her. She buckled up and watched the air hostesses carry out their safety demonstration.

'This is your captain speaking. Welcome onboard this A432 flight to Kos. The weather conditions are clear, and we have a good tailwind to take us down to Greece. Flight time today is approximately four hours twenty minutes.'

Scarlotte listened intently to the captain as the Boeing 737 started to be pushed back from its boarding gate. The journey had begun.

PART ONE

Chapter Five

'Ladies and gentlemen, the captain has now lit up the seatbelt sign. Please return to your seat and securely fasten your seatbelt in preparation for landing.'

Scarlotte was woken from her third doze of the journey by the air hostess's announcement. She removed the dribble from her chin with the back of her hand, tightened her seatbelt and looked out of the window. She could see Kos just below her. It really did look like paradise with the turquoise sea lapping at the coastline of the tiny lush island. The plane would fly over Kos before turning sharply back on itself for its descent to the precariously short runway.

The last time Scarlotte had felt this happy was when she had first driven her green jeep with Joshy in the back purring and kneading the blanket there. This was a different type of happy though - the type you experienced with every atom of your being. She felt warm and fuzzy inside and could not wait to feel the Greek sun on her skin and smell the floral essence of the Kos foliage. Come on, Captain, let's get this show on the road, she thought.

As soon as the aeroplane wheels screeched to a halt on the runway, straining passengers' necks as their heads were jolted forward, the plane erupted into applause as usual.

Oh God, here we go again, Scarlotte thought whilst rummaging under the seat in front of her for her hand luggage. Every passenger scrambled up on their feet, eager to be the first to retrieve their own hand luggage from the overhead lockers. Heads were bashed with falling cases and tempers were frayed as elbows flew around the confined space with people fighting to be the first to depart from the aircraft. She wondered if the airline ever received any claims for whiplash from the landing in Kos, or from the luggage bouncing off their foreheads. *Where there's blame there's a claim* was what the TV adverts advised.

'Bloody hell, calm down,' she murmured. 'We will all get off eventually - and let's face it, we won't be leaving the runway until the bus that transfers us to Arrivals is rammed nose-to-nose full of tourists.'

The arrivals area was an interesting experience at Kos airport. The queues for passport control were long and the air-conditioning was not adequate for the local temperature. Scarlotte could smell the sweaty armpits of the bunch of guys ahead of her in the queue: it was a mixture of alcohol and male sweat which made her feel a bit sick. They looked like they were here on a stag do, as they all wore the same T-shirt proudly displaying *What goes on tour stays on tour* on the front and their nicknames printed on the back. She was standing behind 'Nobby'.

I hope their girlfriends are going somewhere fun too with the same T-shirt logo on the front, she thought to herself as the guys' laughter became louder and louder. They had obviously already had a skinful of beers on the plane and they would surely be a handful in their resort. She hoped they were not going to be on her transfer bus to Kardamena.

*

It was early evening by the time Scarlotte's transfer minibus pulled up outside of the apartment which would be her home for the next week. It was a plain white building surrounded by sandy-gravel pathways. Unlike the last apartment she had stayed in with Eve, it didn't have luxurious well-kept gardens, which was a shame. Still, she would only be sleeping there - or maybe not if she were lucky.

Manoli had already told her that he would not be able to meet her at the apartment as he had to keep his shop open until 10 p.m. That was fine. It gave Scarlotte time to breathe and recover from the journey. She would drop off her bags, check her armpits for body odour and brush her teeth to replace her dog breath with the fresh minty smell of toothpaste. After combing her long blonde fine hair which had knotted at the back of her neck through sweating and also wiping the layer of grease off her forehead, she locked the apartment door behind her and headed into town - a short walk of just 100 metres to the square.

It felt weird being in the resort on her own without her mum, but she raised her chin and strode confidently ahead. She could do this! At the square, she made a quick phone call home to tell Eve that she was safely arrived, and then she set off for Manoli's shop.

Her heart began to race as the shop came into sight. And there he was just inside, neatly folding T-shirts.

'Agapi mou!' Manoli threw his arms into the air and ran out of his shop to embrace Scarlotte. She had no idea what *agapi mou* meant but would soon discover that it was Greek for 'my love'.

'Aw, I'm so happy to be back.' Scarlotte had dreamed about this moment every second of her waking hours for the last couple of weeks. She wrapped her arms around his neck and returned the cuddle, perhaps a little too enthusiastically as Manoli nearly tumbled over. At 5 feet 10 inches, she was ever so slightly taller than Manoli's 5 foot 8. Normally, this would bother her, but she would make an exception for this bloody gorgeous Greek god. He could be 5 feet 5 inches for all she cared. Well, actually no, that would feel just a bit too much like she was dating an Oompa Loompa.

'I have missed you, my darling Scarlotte.' His pronunciation of 'darling' was just delicious: he rolled the r's which was irresistible. Scarlotte released Manoli from her bone-crushing neck grip, not quite the type of grip that her brother would do to her whilst scraping the top of her head hard with his knuckles but not too dissimilar either.

His eyes were alive, his beaming smile wide and his handsome face golden-tanned, just as she remembered. He smelt of the most wonderful spicy aftershave. He had obviously freshened up for her arrival and his hair was ever so slightly damp at the roots from recently washing it. She was in love.

'I have missed you too. The last two weeks have felt so long.' She really meant this from the bottom of her heart. She had never felt like this about anyone else.

They spent the remainder of the evening in Manoli's shop talking about how much they had missed each other and how lucky they were to have met whilst she was on holiday with her mum. They sat by the till on two wooden stools at the back of the small and ever so neat and well-stocked shop. Manoli's hand rested on Scarlotte's knee as they chatted, and he gently stroked her right cheek with the back of his fingers to show his love for her. This made her feel a little embarrassed as no one had ever done that to her before; she usually kept that type of stroking for her cat Joshy's head.

Enthusiastic tourists popped in and out of the shop to browse his wares, some enjoying the last evening of their holiday and keen to use up their drachmas on gifts for friends and family at home. Scarlotte was extremely interested in his wares too – but not the ones displayed on hangers on the shop rails. She could not wait to get her hands on him.

At ten o'clock all of the gift shops along the street began the nightly task of packing away their goods, removing display hangers from outside and neatly storing them away within their shop space. Scarlotte tried her best to help by handing T-shirts, shorts and bikinis to Manoli as he hooked them on the higher shelves in the shop. They would occasionally brush hands as the items were passed along and she felt a tingle of electricity when his warm skin touched hers.

'Are you hungry, agapi mou, shall we eat?' Daft question for Scarlotte really as there was not a minute in the day that she would not need a feed.

'Always!' Rubbing her tummy, Scarlotte was actually really hungry after eating the measly portion of food on the plane. She had never experienced such a thing as love sickness when it came to food and she certainly was not going to start now.

Manoli finished locking up the shop and the two of them walked along the seafront hand-in-hand to a traditional Greek restaurant. The evening breeze was warm on Scarlotte's face and the glow in her heart shone through to her big blue eyes.

The decked dining area, which was next to the beach, was lit up with white fairy-lights. The tables were covered in crisp white linen tablecloths, and each had a little candle and a single fresh flower placed in a tiny blue vase. Greek music played softly in the background, accompanied by the gentle chitter-chatter of diners whilst the waiters, clad in white shirts and black waistcoats, politely served the few guests who were finishing off their meals. The sky was pitch black, allowing the moon and stars to shine brighter than Scarlotte had ever seen them before. The sea was calm and alongside the soft music you could hear the soothing sound of waves lapping at the shore.

Manoli was greeted by the restaurant owner whom he obviously knew well. When introductions were over, they were seated at the best spot in the restaurant by the beach edge. Scarlotte hadn't noticed this place when she was on holiday with her mum; it seemed less touristy and more a place for the locals. She was pleased that there was not a British football shirt in sight.

'What would you like to eat, agapi mou?' Manoli was leaning over the table towards Scarlotte, holding her hands in his. He was even more handsome than had remembered, and she really couldn't believe that she had bagged such a spunky guy.

'You choose, please. I would like to eat something that

you would enjoy.' Scarlotte was a little embarrassed that she had yet to get to really understand the local cuisine as most of the dishes she had eaten whilst on holiday with Mum had involved those everlasting chips. Hopefully, by getting Manoli to choose she wouldn't show herself up by revealing that she really didn't have a scooby doo.

Their handsome waiter Takis delivered an array of wonderful dishes for what was called a Greek Meze. Scarlotte knew she really must stop sneaking looks at him, but she couldn't help herself. There wasn't anything wrong with window-shopping, was there? The men on Kos were so different and so much more attractive than the ones at home.

They ate stuffed dolmades, tzatziki, tender beef stew and freshly baked bread all washed down with a small glass of Greek white wine which tasted to Scarlotte like watered-down vinegar. Her face screwed up as if she had just bitten into a lemon as she sipped the wine, but she told Manoli that she did in fact like it. He wasn't a big drinker, and as he slowly sipped at his vinegar, Scarlotte wondered if it would be rude to order a large one - or perhaps she would get a large one later, she giggled to herself!

After Manoli had paid for the meal they took the walk along the beach to Scarlotte's apartment which would be home for the next week. They removed their shoes and tiptoed hand-in-hand to the water's edge. Manoli took Scarlotte in his arms.

'I am so happy that you are here, agapi mou.' He gazed into her eyes, pulled her closer and kissed her passionately on the lips. She could feel a rush of heat creep up her neck. They both wanted each other desperately but the beach certainly was not the right place for them to consummate their love.

Chapter Six

The next morning Scarlotte was woken up at 6 a.m. by the local alarm clock. 'Bloody cockerels - go back to sleep!' she grumbled. She hadn't got to bed until one o'clock and needed her beauty sleep.

To her surprise, last night Manoli had been a complete gentleman. He had walked her home, kissed her sweetly on the cheek and bade her goodnight. To be honest, she was relieved because she was too knackered to be performing any bedroom acrobatics after her long journey.

After dozing off again for a couple of hours, Scarlotte dragged herself out of bed and opened the blackout curtains. She squinted and covered her eyes with her arm as the sun blasted its light and heat into the room. The sky was the bluest sky she had ever seen, not like the polluted skies of the UK. Today was going to be a beach day for sure and perhaps every day from now on!

She unpacked her rucksack and hung her creased clothes neatly in the old wooden wardrobe then put her towel, suntan lotion and book in her white linen beach bag for a day by the sea. She wore her best new white bikini with the pearlescent sequins stitched onto the boob area, a mini-skirt and a plain white T-shirt. Wedge sandals were the choice of footwear today and would give her another couple of inches on her height. She loved being the tallest girl around; you could get a bird's-eye view in any crowd. Great when checking out the local talent, she smirked to herself, before feeling guilty at the thought.

Peckish as always, she stopped off in the local patisserie in the square and treated herself to a sugary pastry and a coffee. The pastry was still warm when she took her first bite, and it melted in her mouth. Bloody lovely it was! With coffee in hand and after swiping the crumbs from her chin she strolled down to Manoli's shop to say hi to him before spending the next few hours on the beach.

'Good morning, how are you today?' she greeted him as she strode into the shop. It didn't have normal doors, just large patio-type ones that had to be lifted out of their sockets and pushed back in order to make a doorway.

'Ah, agapi mou! Did you sleep well?' Manoli wrapped his arms around her waist and kissed her hard on the lips. Scarlotte noticed that she had transferred a piece of her pastry onto Manoli's top lip and laughed as she gently brushed it off.

'Sorry! I hope you like pastry - I saved you that bit.' She thought it was funny but the humour obviously did not translate into Greek. She should really try to talk a little slower so he could better understand her. His English was reasonable, but it wasn't strong enough for him to get her silly sense of humour.

'Would you like some yoghurt and honey, agapi mou?' he asked now.

'Yes, please, that sounds lovely.' Scarlotte was already full from her pastry but she hadn't mastered the art of refusing food.

Looking as fresh and gorgeous as usual, Manoli quickly produced two white plastic bowls from under the till, a tub of Greek natural yoghurt, a bag of mixed nuts and a jar of local honey. He confidently made the breakfast for them both whilst she wandered around the shop checking out which item she would choose first if she was buying. Spotting a green and blue patterned bikini with a gold ring at the front of the bra top and at the side of the bottoms, she picked it up and held it against her body.

'Take it, agapi mou, it will suit you.' Manoli came behind her and kissed her neck. She wished he wouldn't because it sent sparks down her spine and she really did not need to be getting sweaty at this hour of the morning.

'No, Manoli, I can't just take it. I will pay for it.'

42

Secretly, she would of course have liked it for free but that would be taking advantage . . . wouldn't it?

'It is my gift for you arriving. Please, you must take it,' he insisted as he took the bikini off the hanger and placed it in her beach bag. Scarlotte felt quite emotional at his kind gesture and felt a prick of tears appear in her eyes. Noticing this, Manoli kissed her on the cheek, saying gently, 'Come, eat your breakfast.'

Scarlotte ate really fast and sometimes thought she could easily enter a cream-cracker- eating contest and thrash the opposition. She polished off her yoghurt well before Manoli and sat restlessly waiting for him to finish. She didn't have a lot of patience and quickly became anxious to head off to the beach for some sun.

'I might go to the beach now for a while, do you mind?' If he did, she would go anyway.

'Of course, please go and enjoy your first day. Come and meet me later for food and coffee.' God, she didn't really want to interrupt her day on the beach to have coffee, but as it was Manoli she would make an exception. However, she would certainly not be making a habit of it just yet.

They kissed each other and Manoli held onto her hand as she left the shop.

'See you later,' she said, and turned around and waved as he watched her stride away.

Scarlotte was free to roam on her own, which she loved. She was more than happy in her own company and didn't feel the need to have people around her all of the time. As a child she had been painfully shy, but now at twenty-two years of age, she was really beginning to grow in confidence. After all, she had come to Greece on her own which took some balls, she thought, and felt enormously proud of herself. Chin in the air, she marched down the street to the beach, unaware of the blond guy in the shop opposite Manoli's staring at her as she passed by his window.

Chapter Seven

It was seven o'clock and tonight would be the first proper full evening of her adventure. Scarlotte got herself in the shower to wash off the sand which had made its way into all sorts of places that it really should not. She had to turn the heat of the water down to a cool setting because her back was bright red from the sun and the water felt like little needles pricking her skin. She wriggled around in the shower until she could bear the heat. It was lovely being on your own on the beach, but the only downside was that it was really tricky to put suntan lotion on your back without looking like you were performing a contortionist's act. Although she'd only recently been in Kardamena with her mum, her tan had quickly faded and her skin needed plenty of protection.

I don't really want to just go and sit in the shop with Manoli all night, she decided as she locked the door to her apartment. Feeling fresh and good about her appearance, she took the long route down to his shop, cutting through a path that would take her along the seafront. The street was lined with cocktail bars with flowery cushions placed on wicker chairs which were strategically placed to face the sea. It was quite busy along the front and there were lots of tanned couples enjoying a pre-dinner drink before seeking a restaurant to enjoy a Greek delicacy of some sort - with chips, of course.

Should she stop for a drink or would she just look like a saddo loner? Whilst she was confident in herself, she didn't fancy the thought of anyone making assumptions about her based on her being in a bar on her own. People were always making instant judgments about others - and quite often those judgments were far from accurate. Deciding that she wouldn't let that stop her, Scarlotte walked into the next bar along.

'A Pina Colado, please.' After browsing the cocktail menu, she didn't think that ordering Sex on the Beach or a Screaming Orgasm were appropriate choices for a young lady on her own. She wished at that moment that her friend Lisa was there too as she would definitely order the raciest named cocktail on the menu.

The waiter hadn't been blessed with the handsome looks of Manoli, but she still fluttered her mascara-laden eyelashes at him and showed off her ever-so white smile since at home this would often result in a free cocktail chaser.

The cocktail arrived in a large glass covered with fruit and of course the obligatory sparkler. Bother. There was no way that she would be able to remain low-profile with Guy Fawkes delivering a fireworks display to her table. Jealous onlookers watched as Scarlotte was presented with the massive cocktail. She felt a blush rise up her neck and wondered whether this was actually one of her best ideas. It wasn't. She would soon learn that the Greek people on this island were very gossipy and that this pit-stop for a cocktail would certainly make its way back to Manoli. Although that wouldn't normally bother her, she knew she had to be on her best behaviour with her new man, especially as she would be moving in with him in a week's time.

Feeling a little tipsy after her Ouzo cocktail chaser, she continued her walk along the seafront. There were hundreds of young holidaymakers out by now, all drinking a mishmash of cocktails, beer, Diamond White and Castaway.

'Hello, lovely lady, come and join us for a drink!' English PR staff were like herders, trying to get every passing person into their bar. Music was playing loudly and you had to shout your 'Maybe after I've eaten' response back, which was the only way of getting past them.

One of the guys was extra-persistent; he was a PR for a

bar called Blue & White. He wore blue and white striped jeans and a yellow fitted T-shirt which made him look like a stick of rock. He was tall, about 6 feet, with slightly receding spiky fair hair and a sun-exposed face which gave his skin the appearance of soft leather. 'Come on, darlin', come and have a drink with us. You look like you could do with a shot of tequila or maybe an Orgasm!' Greg, as he introduced himself, was a scouser – from Liverpool, of course. Scarlotte loved a scouse accent and instantly liked him, and his cheeky grin.

'I can't tonight, I'm just off to meet someone.' She could have said that she was going to meet her boyfriend but that would potentially be limiting her chances of fun on the island. Normally she would be straight in the bar necking the tequila shots like the rest of them, but she really needed to hold back tonight. She bade Greg farewell and promised to come back another night. He then swiftly moved on to terrorise the next unsuspecting passers-by.

Fighting her way through the crowds and the clutches of fun-loving, sun-kissed male and female PRs, she cut through a short street which led to the row of shops where Manoli's shop was situated.

'Ah, agapi mou, I missed you,' he said on seeing her.

Scarlotte frowned to herself. She had only seen him a few hours ago for lunch and coffee, for heaven's sake. Was he going to be intense and clingy? She hoped not because the first sign of control from a guy instantly put her off. Pushing the thought aside, she gave him a big cuddle and a kiss. She had sucked a mint to disguise the Pina Colada smell on her breath. She didn't want him to think that she was one of those drunken English tourists who frequented the resort, although the thought of hanging out with those folks on the front was very appealing.

Scarlotte soon grew bored of helping customers to find their perfect T-shirt size and longed for another Pina Colada down on the front with the other English holidaymakers.

Plonking herself down on the stool at the back of the shop she started to think about the coming weeks and came to the conclusion that she should really find herself a job in order to maintain her independence.

'Manoli, I need to get a job whilst I'm here,' she announced as he waved off another happy customer.

'No, agapi mou, you don't need to. You can help me in the shop.' How could she resist that perfect smile? He came and sat next to her and stroked her cheek, making her feel like a pet again.

'But I need my own money.' The thought of having to ask Manoli for money to purchase tampons made her squirm. She wasn't sure that he would even know the word 'tampon' in English and sniggered inwardly at the thought of having to try to explain by using the power of mime, pointing at her lady bits and pretending to insert a tampon. No no no, it was going to be too difficult; she absolutely needed to earn her own money.

It was agreed that after her first week's holiday and when she had moved in with Manoli, she would help in the shop from 10 a.m. until 2 p.m. some days and 4 p.m. until 10 p.m. the other days. She wasn't too happy at having to work in the daytime, but with the endless sunshine here, she would still be able to have many hours on the beach.

Manoli said he would take her jet-skiing the following morning. His friend owned several jet-skis and they could use them for free.

'How exciting, I can't wait!'

'You will love it, agapi mou. I will teach you.'

This night was far from over though. They wouldn't go for a meal after the shop had closed, they would eat something back at Scarlotte's apartment. She knew exactly where this was going to lead to and imagined herself limbering up like a gymnast ready for a night of fun.

After closing the shop, they bought chicken kebabs from a café in the square to take back with them. The smell of freshly barbecued chicken with salad and tzatziki made Scarlotte's mouth water and she could have quite easily demolished the whole lot there and then.

'I want you, agapi mou,' he whispered passionately into her ear. And right now I want my kebab, she thought, and bit her lip at the thought that it would go cold and uneaten on the kitchenette work surface.

Scarlotte unlocked her apartment door with Manoli so close behind her that she could feel his need for her pressing into her leg. She would not be getting much sleep, or food tonight – even though both of these were actually two of her favourite things in the world. Secretly, she much preferred them to becoming a sweaty, sticky mess in bed.

Manoli left around two o'clock in the morning as he needed to be up at eight to prepare the shop for opening. The tourist season only lasted six months, and every hour of it must be used to make money to tide the island families over the autumn and winter until the shops re-opened in the April of the following year. So - there was no time to slack off during the height of the holiday season.

Scarlotte herself had stayed in bed until ten o'clock today; she was tired and hungry and considered eating the cold kebab still standing untouched on the sideboard. Then she reluctantly changed her mind. It was probably best not to risk giving herself food poisoning and ending up with the plippety-plops, she thought as she quickly showered and tried on her new bikini from Manoli's shop. She would go to the pastry shop instead for something sugary and a coffee on the way to the beach.

*

The first week passed by quickly with much of the same daily routine. Scarlotte would need to pack today, ready to move her things into Manoli's place. He had taken her to see the apartment yesterday which was situated just a short walk from his shop. The place was quite small, Scarlotte saw, and was very plain with just a bed on the far wall, a single wardrobe and a small kitchenette area. There wasn't much natural light apart from a small sliding window on the right wall. It was OK though; she didn't plan on spending much time there anyway.

'Where shall I hang my clothes - is there room in the wardrobe?' Manoli had cleared half the wardrobe already for her stuff. She was planning to take a bag of clothes to the local launderette later today as she had worn most of her holiday wear, which was now scrunched up in her rucksack.

The launderette was not a typical-style place like you got in the UK. It was basically an elderly Greek lady who would take your bag of dirty knickers, wash them and hang them for all and sundry to see on one of the mass of washing lines in her front garden. Apart from not ironing them, she did a good job of removing every speck of dirt off your clothes and they always smelt lovely and fresh from being dried in the Greek sunshine.

Manoli left Scarlotte to settle in, as he needed to get back to the shop which was being looked after by the guy who owned the shop opposite. Once satisfied that she had crammed her stuff into the wardrobe and filled a carrier bag with dirty washing, Scarlotte went off to the shops to buy a phone card to call her mum. She had only called Eve once since arriving and she felt a strong need to hear her mum's voice.

'Hello, darling daughter! How are you? How's it going? How's Manoli? What is his apartment like? Are you getting your tan back?' So many questions and so much to talk about! They spent the maximum phone-card allowance of 5 drachma enjoying chatting to each other.

'You have a letter here,' her mum said. 'Shall I open it for you?'

'Yes, please.' Scarlotte could hear Eve tearing open the envelope as the phone card dropped down to its last drachma.

'Oh, it's a job offer from the airport!' In all the

excitement of her new adventure, Scarlotte had completely forgotten about the interview she had had two months ago for the position of Airport Police Officer. It was a really good job and the money was good too. The letter was asking Scarlotte to start in three weeks' time.

'Bloody hell, Mum, what should I do?! Mum . . . Mum?' Eve was about to reply when the phone card ran out, leaving just a bleeping tone in Scarlotte's ear. Frustrated at not hearing her mum's advice, she accepted that she would have some proper grown-up decisions to make on her own for now.

Chapter Eight

'I think you should go for it, agapi mou. It sounds like a really great job for you.'

Scarlotte was sitting next to Manoli at the back of his shop, feeling very confused about which direction her life should take. Should she stay in Greece with no certain job but a life with the gorgeous Manoli, or should she go back to England and train for a new position as an Airport Police Officer. It was breaking her heart to think of leaving so soon, but she was fiercely independent and the prospect of a secure job back at home was also very appealing.

'I don't know what to do,' she told him. 'I love being here with you, but it is a great opportunity. My friend already works there, and she loves it.' Scarlotte felt a prick of tears touch her eyes at the thought of leaving Kardamena; she looked up to the ceiling and blinked to stop the droplets from falling. But she had to admit that she did feel some excitement at having been offered this fantastic position in a brand new and fascinating career back at home.

Over the next few days, they discussed her decision, and after much deliberation and with input from her mum, Scarlotte decided to leave Kos and return to the UK to start the police job. She would fly home a week on Friday and start the new job on the following Monday. The return flight was booked by her mum, so her decision had now reached the point of no return.

Scarlotte and Manoli spent all of their time together over the last week of her stay. He had taken her jet-skiing again and frightened the life out of her when she rode pillion whilst he performed 'doughnuts' in the deep sea - it was exhilarating. They made love, they ate at good restaurants and even went to Manoli's friend's nightclub Tropical for a dance. It was blissful and fun, and Scarlotte was still not convinced that she was making the right life decision.

'Agapi mou, I will miss you so much.' Manoli felt his heart tighten at the prospect of his new love leaving him but he would remain strong in front of her.

'Can I come back if I don't like the job? I don't know if I'm doing the right thing, and I will miss you too much.' Scarlotte was desperate to keep her options open with Manoli, even though she knew it was not fair to ask him to wait around for her. It definitely wouldn't take long for him to be snapped up by another girl, that was for sure.

'Yes, darling, I will call you each day so you can tell me what you are thinking.' Manoli pulled Scarlotte towards him and embraced her tightly. He was actually so easygoing and did not try to control her as she had first thought he might. He genuinely wanted her to be happy in whichever direction her life took her. He was a kind soul.

Another goodbye to contend with made Scarlotte feel a little anxious. She asked Manoli not to go to the airport with her, which would make the departure a little easier for them both. They spent their last evening together which was magical but also deeply upsetting. Scarlotte was fearful: had she made a massive mistake?

Chapter Nine

The skies were grey and clouds bursting with rain as the aeroplane pulled to a stop at the Nottingham airport. Scarlotte felt instantly depressed and cold as she pulled the neck up on her denim jacket and wrapped her arms around herself. She was shivering in her shorts and realised how stupid she'd been for not putting on her jeans and boots. Her usual zest for life and twinkle in her eye seemed to have faded and she felt like her heart was crying inside of her.

'All right, love?' Her dad Roger had come to collect her from the airport. He could tell that his daughter was sad and gave her a big kiss on the cheek before loading her rucksack into the back of his car.

'Congratulations on getting the new job, lass, you've done very well for yourself. I'm proud of you. Are you excited?'

'Thanks, Dad, but I don't know. I am excited, yes, but the trouble is, I also loved it in Greece.' The weather certainly did not help her mood. She had just left sunny skies and 70-degree heat to come back to this miserable weather which just made the whole prospect of being home miserable too.

The journey back to Eve's house took longer than normal due to the torrential rain slowing traffic on the motorway. Scarlotte stared out of the car window hardly talking because she was so mixed up in her head right now. Rain pelted against the windscreen as her dad put the wipers on super-fast mode.

'You'll be fine, love, once you start the job. It's something you've wanted to do for a long time and you'll be really good at it.' Roger's words of comfort and encouragement did make her feel a little better but it was still going to be hard to be upbeat.

They reached the house and Roger helped his daughter to the door, carrying her big backpack for her. After giving her a kiss and saying hello to his former wife, he dashed off through the rain back to the car to return to work.

'Hello, darling daughter. Welcome home.' Eve was pleased as Punch to have her little girl home and safe again, and had of course put a large piece of lamb in the oven. She gave Scarlotte a big cuddle then went to make a cup of tea for them.

'How are you feeling about being back and have you told Lisa you're home?' Eve shouted from the kitchen as she filled the kettle.

'I don't know, Mum. I've not spoken to Lisa, but I will' Scarlotte's voice began to shake and she knew that she would burst into tears any minute. She had been talking to herself all the way back from the airport, muttering, 'Don't cry, don't cry, don't cry.' But she knew she would as soon as she started talking to her mum.

Eve quickly came back into the front room, sat next to Scarlotte on the sofa and put her arm around her shoulder.

'Go back to Greece if you want to,' she said gently. 'Don't worry about what anyone else says. It's your life so you go and do what you want. You'll always be able to get another job if you decide to come home again.'

This was the green light that Scarlotte had needed. She had thought that her mum might have wanted her to take the sensible option to come home and start the police job, but Eve was always supportive, and above all else she wanted her child to be happy no matter what she did. She could clearly see that Scarlotte's heart was breaking and that just would not do.

The following day, a flight was booked back to Kos. Scarlotte wrote an apologetic letter to explain that she was unable after all to take the job with the Airport Police. Being back in the rainy UK had given her a massive reality check. Life was short and she wanted to make the most of it.

'Oh my God, agapi mou! You have made me a very happy man.' Scarlotte could literally see the smile on Manoli's face as she spoke to him on the phone. 'I will collect you from the airport.'

Manoli had phoned that night and Scarlotte could not wait to tell him that her life was destined to be with him in Kos, not in this depressing country. The twinkle in her eye was rekindled and this new decision had lifted a massive weight off her shoulders. Her adventure in Kardamena would now be able to continue. And she would be sure to put her whole heart and soul into this second chance at happiness.

PART TWO

Chapter Ten

Scarlotte could see what looked like a Scooby Doo van waiting outside at the pick-up area of Kos airport. That looks really funky, she thought. She scanned the crowded Arrivals area for Manoli. New tourists were buzzing around trying to find their transfer coaches as reps with clipboards at the ready were desperately attempting to herd the excited holidaymakers into buses. It was early evening and the sun was still hot; she could feel the sweat dripping down her back which actually felt really good after the chilly weather back in the Midlands.

'Agapi mou! Over here!' Bloody hell, it was Scooby Doo and Scrappy Doo who had come to collect her! Manoli leapt out of the passenger seat of the funky van like an excited puppy. She noticed it was actually covered in flowers with a big *Tropical Club* sign nestled in the middle of the hand-painted foliage. Scarlotte felt really cool as onlookers watched the Greek god meet her and throw her rucksack into the back of the van.

Manoli's friend who owned the nightclub had kindly brought Manoli to collect Scarlotte. She learned that his name was Panos. He was such a lovely guy, really friendly and kind. He was much taller than Manoli and good-looking in a quirky way, in his faded T-shirt, board shorts and orange flipflops which had seen better days. Scarlotte thought he looked like a surfer with his messy mop of curly thick hair.

'Welcome home, darrrling.' Manoli rolled his r's in that sexy way that he always did. She squeezed in the middle front seat between the two guys and held tightly onto Manoli's hand. She felt wonderful again and knew at this moment that she had made the right decision. This really did feel like home for her now with the gorgeous flowery smell of the air, the warmth of the sun and the familiar surroundings of white and blue quaint Greek houses which lined the road to the resort.

When back at Manoli's apartment, Scarlotte was left alone to settle in and unpack again as Manoli went off to tend to his customers at the shop. As she hung up her clothes, she wondered if he had been with any other girls whilst she'd been away. Scarlotte could be fiercely jealous at times and could not help but check his pillowcases for signs of hairs which did not belong to Manoli. Feeling a little guilty for snooping, she sniffed around and checked drawers and bathroom for signs of another woman.

With her heart beating fast at the horrible thought of finding something suspicious or worse - at Manoli returning unexpectedly to find her in the act of rooting around - she made herself stop and sat on the bed. I would have made a good police officer, she thought, maybe even working in forensics. Then: 'God, I need to get a grip,' she said out loud as she lay down on the bed exhausted from the journey and from her jealousy. She had no idea why she had this jealous streak and why she found it so hard to trust men. Would she, in fact, ever be able to trust a man completely? Perhaps she should go and see a psychiatrist to try to find the root cause of the problem.

After dozing on the bed for an hour, Scarlotte began to feel hungry. She made herself look presentable and headed out. There was a jacket-potato place called Philip's just off the square and feeling the need for a massive carb-fix, she navigated straight towards it. She asked for cheese and beans, her favourite jacket potato fillings, since they would melt the butter into a lovely gooey mess. At Philip's they baked the potatoes properly, in the oven, not like those microwaved crap ones which left the skin just floppy and soggy. This one had lovely crispy skin, the type that would often snap your plastic fork.

Picking up the last bit of potato skin with her fingers and

shoving it in her mouth, she walked towards Manoli's shop. She could see the fair-haired guy from the shop opposite hovering outside of his doorway. 'Good evening, welcome back,' he called out, as if he knew her, but she had never really seen much of him before. Then she remembered how gossipy this town was and was sure that everyone knew that she had left and then come back.

'Oh, er thanks,' she replied as a baked bean fell off the potato skin and onto her white T-shirt. I'm such a classy bird, she thought as she flicked it off, narrowly missing the guy's left trainer. 'Ooops, sorry about that,' she giggled awkwardly as she threw the foil potato tray into the bin outside the ice-cream parlour next to his shop.

'No problem, gorgeous lady. You can flick your bean at me anytime.'

No innuendo intended, she thought at his cheeky comment.

Blondie boy had a Greek accent but looked more Scandinavian. He was about the same height as Scarlotte and had piercing blue eyes set in the middle of a broad, golden-tanned face. His top teeth were white and straight but somehow a bit too big for his mouth. Scarlotte thought he was attractive in a goofy sort of way.

Half-ignoring him after his bean-flicking comment, she quickly walked across the street to Manoli's shop. He was inside hanging up some new T-shirts that she knew he would have recently purchased from the wholesalers in Kos Town.

'Who is that guy opposite, Manoli?' she asked. 'Is he your friend?'

'Not really a friend, agapi mou. He just watches the shop for me sometimes if I need to go out.'

Manoli didn't have too many friends yet in Kos. He was originally from Athens and had come to the island to start his business just last year. It seemed though that those friends that he did have were, like Panos, were good and loyal pals to him.

'Why do you ask?' Manoli wanted to know.

'No reason. I just wondered if you were friends, that's all.' She wouldn't tell him about the bean exchange for fear that he might be cross with Blondie Boy.

*

Scarlotte settled back into Greek island life well and was amazed at how many people had welcomed her back to Kos. Perhaps it was just the local rumour-mill again doing its work.

Over the next few days, it was as though she had never been away. She helped Manoli in the shop, covering for him whilst he went to the wholesalers, went for a swim or popped home for his shower. He was never too far away if she needed him. She was so proud of herself if she made a sale in Manoli's absence and he would give her a big cuddle for her efforts.

Manoli had purchased one of those tiny little motorbikes whilst she had been away and he would zip around the town, expertly weaving in and out of people walking on the main shopping street. Scarlotte would often ride pillion, gripping onto Manoli's waist for safety. It was really good fun and she loved to feel the wind rushing through her hair. You didn't need to wear a helmet on the island which made the experience even more exhilarating.

'Can you teach me to ride the bike?' She was a good car driver, so she thought that this would also be a doddle.

'Yes, of course,' he replied generously. 'We will go to a quiet place tomorrow morning and I will show you.'

Well, that was a mistake! They had gotten up early the following morning and headed to an old piece of bumpy wasteland. It was not the best place for a novice Hells Angel to learn her biking skills. Scarlotte's gangly legs seemed to get in the way each time she tried to move the bike; she felt nervous about picking them up off the ground to actually allow the bike to move. It took a good ten goes for her to finally move about two metres without using her legs as stabilizers.

'Woo-hoo!! Did you see that, Manoli?' she screeched. 'I did it!'

He clapped and walked the whole two metres to give her a kiss. 'Now try again, agapi mou - but this time keep your feet on the footrests.'

Scarlotte put the bike back into first gear with her flipflopped foot - very unsuitable footwear for a Hells Angel trainee - and gave the bike some welly. Flying off at what felt 100mph, she whizzed around the wasteland like a real pro.

'Ha ha! I love it!' she shouted. She slowed a little to make a turn at the opposite end of the wasteland and more slowly this time, she rode back towards Manoli.

BANG! The back tyre burst, having gone over a sharp bit of gravel. The bike wobbled precariously from side to side, not helped by Scarlotte's legs flying everywhere. Her heart was racing as she tried desperately to control the bike. A flipflop flew off her foot, narrowly missing Manoli's left ear as he ran towards her like a knight in shining armour.

'Agapi mou!! Are you OK?' He managed to catch her just before the bike fell onto the ground.

Breathless from the excitement, she threw her arms around him as he whipped her out of danger. 'Yes, I'm fine - I think,' she gasped, and then she burst into uncontrollable fits of laughter. Tears were running down her face and she almost peed herself. She would not be riding the bike anytime soon, especially now that she'd broken it.

Chapter Eleven

It was early evening and Scarlotte fancied a walk before she headed off to the shop to help Manoli. Her skin was golden-brown again now and her hair was even blonder from the sunshine, giving it that lovely sun-kissed look. She felt good in herself but not like one of those people who really knew that they were great-looking. She would barely notice the stares from guys as she walked past them on the street.

'Ooh, a shoe shop.' She hadn't spotted this little gem before and wondered if it was in fact a mirage. The tiny shop was buried deep within the back streets of the resort and surely wouldn't get much trade nestled back there . . . until now, of course!

There were trendy flipflops, heels to die for, and an array of wedges. Scarlotte felt like she had died and gone to heaven. Eyes wide with interest, she spotted a pair that seemed to be winking at her, silently calling: *'Take me home! Take me home, please.'* She often found that beautiful shoes did this, which was why she had a million pairs.

The sandals had a small wooden block heel, about two inches high; the open-toe front was soft black suede with a lace fastening, a bit like an old-fashioned roller skate, and a buckle around the ankle-strap. They were bloody beautiful, and she just *had* to have them. The problem was that she didn't have any spare cash right now as she had spent most of her savings on flights back and forth to Kos. She had a bit left, but she would need that to buy a flight back in June for her brother's wedding.

Feeling somewhat disappointed she drooped all the way back to the shop.

To his credit, Manoli noticed immediately. 'What's the matter, agapi mou?' he asked. 'You look sad tonight.'

'I'm OK. I've just seen the most amazing pair of shoes, that's all, but I can't afford them.'

Manoli laughed and gave her a hug. 'Here, take this money and go and buy them for yourself.' He handed her a wedge of cash out of his jeans pocket.

'No, I can't do that. I've always had my own money and I feel bad.' Inside though she felt her mood rise instantly as the prospect of putting those bad boy sandals on her golden-brown tootsies.

'Please, Scarlotte, you work hard here, you must take the money.'

Quicker than a Venus Flytrap catches its prey, she whipped the cash out of his hand and marched back to the shop. 'Please have my size,' she prayed. She took a size 40. If they only had a 39, she would make her feet fit in them if it killed her.

In less than ten minutes later she walked out of the shop beaming all over her face. Amazing, wasn't it, how a pair of shoes could bring such pleasure. She loved them and was delighted that they did have her size and that she wouldn't have to cripple herself in a smaller pair.

Trying them on back at Manoli's shop, she stalked up and down, her hand on her hip like a catwalk model, to display her new purchases to him. She had learned how to move like this at modelling school when she was eighteen; at the end of the course she had had to prance up and down the stage at the local nightclub for her passing-out parade.

'They suit you, agapi mou,' Manoli said as she joyfully showed off her beautiful new shoes.

Then a group of four holidaymakers interrupted her fashion show and needed to be tended to by Manoli. Feeling mildly put out, Scarlotte decided to take a little walk around the town to ensure that the new shoes were comfy – and, of course, to show them off to all and sundry.

Despite the slight pinch on her left little toe she chose to stroll along the main street where all of the young holidaymakers would be having fun. She would definitely need a plaster on that toe later as her left foot was slightly bigger than her right and always gave her gyp when wearing in a new pair of shoes. Most of her friends had one foot bigger than the other and she wondered why shops didn't sell odd sizes to accommodate this. Now *there* was a business idea for the future . . .

She often had ideas of inventing some random piece of equipment to solve a problem. Her best idea, she thought, was to make a tank to carry on your back with a hose-pipe attached. You would fill it with suntan lotion and then spray sunbathers on the beach for a small fee. She would look like a character in a *Ghostbusters* movie, which was a pretty cool look, she thought.

'Hey, foxy lady, surely tonight is the night you come and join us for a drink?' It was Greg doing his herding job again, trying to get the ladies into the bar. He was really good actually and very persuasive - she could see why he was known to be the best PR in the resort.

'Hi Greg, how's it going?' she asked.

'Good, thanks, darlin'. And how's it going with you - in the shop with your boyfriend?' The usual word of mouth had of course spread her relationship with Manoli throughout the resort.

'Yeah, it's OK, thanks. I get a little bit bored sitting there when it's quiet but it's definitely better than being back at home in rainy Nottingham.'

There was a group of girls next to them drinking shots. They were sitting on the comfy flowered seats overlooking the sea.

'Hey, are you from Nottingham then? Me too. I'm Julie.' A tall skinny blonde girl jumped up from the group and came over to introduce herself. She was naturally pretty with a heart-shaped face and blue-grey eyes. Her hair was a slightly darker blonde than Scarlotte's, but the same length and she wore it in a cool surfer-like messy way. Her ripped denim shorts and yellow vest top clung to her boy-like gangly figure.

Scarlotte instantly warmed to Julie and enjoyed a good old girlie chat. They found that they lived only a few miles from each other at home, and Scarlotte learned that Julie was also working in Kos in a take-away in the next street from Manoli's shop. It was only a greasy kebab shop, she explained, but the job paid the rent.

'Hey, fancy coming out for a drink one night?' she suggested.

'Yeah, that would be cool.' Scarlotte brightened up. 'I've not been out since I've been here with Manoli.'

'Really? OK, girl, let's go out tomorrow night, it's my night off. I'll meet you here at eight p.m.'

So, the date was set and all she had to do now was choose what to wear and, of course, break the news to Manoli. She hoped that he wouldn't mind her going out but didn't know how he would react to her coming home after a skinful of the powerful combination of Diamond White cider and Castaway, a white-wine alcopop.

*

Scarlotte had chosen to wear her black leather trousers and her black, long-sleeved top. Naturally she also had on her new shoes with a plaster strategically placed on her left little toe. She had a spare plaster in her pocket just in case it wiggled its way free. Her choker necklace with the black silk ribbon tie and silver starfish would complete her outfit. She was so excited about her first proper night out since coming back to Kardamena.

Manoli had been surprisingly supportive and made sure she had her spare key.

'See you later, darling, don't wait up!' Scarlotte told him.

Manoli was secretly excited at the prospect of his girlfriend coming home a little bit tipsy and no doubt amorous. He would be waiting up for her!

'See you later, agapi mou, have fun.'

Julie was chatting and laughing with Greg when Scarlotte arrived dead on eight o'clock. True to form, she was never late for anything and certainly would not be late for a night on the tiles.

'How you doin', darlin'?'

'Good, thanks, Greg.'

Julie looked lovely. She wore a pair of stone-washed blue skinny jeans and a white vest top. Her hair was freshly washed, blown straight and it shone golden blonde. Julie didn't wear any make-up; she didn't need it because she was naturally pretty. Scarlotte had just applied a bit of mascara and some clear lip gloss.

Greg went to the bar and got them both a complimentary cocktail to start their evening. The blue liquid tasted rank, Scarlotte thought, and was sweeter than eating sugar directly off a spoon.

'Jesus, Greg! What the hell is that?' Scarlotte shuddered and almost spat the drink out. But like a good sport she held her nose and swallowed some of it down.

'Ha ha. I got the barman to make it especially for your first night out.'

'Thanks, Greg, it's really delicious – *not*. Do you want me to be sick? Can I just have a bottle of Castaway for now, please?' The drink wasn't particularly potent and she wanted to start the night off slowly if they were to make it to a club later.

'I quite like it - I'll drink yours.' Julie swiftly necked her own blue poison then took Scarlotte's glass out of her hand and took another big swig. Scarlotte pulled a face and asked her new friend how she could bear to put that disgusting liquid into her body.

'I'll drink owt, duck,' she replied in her Nottingham accent. 'Duck' or 'Ducky' was a Nottingham term of endearment which was used to replace the word 'mate'. A bit like the way Nottingham people called a bread roll a cob, which was always a subject for debate with people from outside. 'It's a roll.' 'No, it's a cob.' 'It's a bap.' 'No, it's a cob.' 'It's a barm cake.' 'No, it's a cob.' A barm cake? What kind of name was that for a cob anyway!

After listening and jigging around to a Bad Manners song at Greg's place, they moved on down the front strip to Poppers Bar. Poppers was the most popular bar on the front, and it was packed outside with groups of guys and girls drinking and generally having a good time on their holiday.

'Let's find a PR to get us a drink,' Julie said. 'What do you fancy?'

'I think I'll have a Blastaway now.' Scarlotte liked the mix of Diamond White with Castaway: the combination was a new trendy drink called a Blastaway. It was quite lethal though and unless you wanted to end up on your back on the floor, you should limit yourself to a couple.

They spent a couple of hours outside Poppers chatting with groups of guys and girls and dancing to the latest chart tunes being played out of the large speakers of the bar. Scarlotte was in her element and was given many offers of drinks from English guys on holiday. She was feeling really good and realising just how much she had missed nights out like this.

At midnight all of the bars had to either turn off their music or move their customers inside to soundproofed areas. The police would patrol the streets just after midnight to ensure that music wasn't still being played and disturbing the local residents. A hefty fine could be given if the rules were broken, so the bars were extremely strict about stopping the music dead on midnight.

Feeling quite tipsy by now, the two girls made the walk up the hill to the largest club called Stars. Scarlotte had only been to Tropical with Manoli; it was a good club, but Stars was the place that most holidaymakers went to. Being recognised as 'locals' at the door, they could enter the club free of charge. The place was huge, and it was packed with people dancing around and flirting with each other. Some girls and guys had already hooked up and were snogging in the middle of the dancefloor whilst trying to perform their dirty dancing moves.

'Crikey, they need to get a room,' Julie laughed as they passed a couple frolicking in a corner.

After getting a drink from the bar, which was also free for them, they headed off with their drinks in hand to the dancefloor. Pop tunes blared out of the speakers which made it impossible to talk to each other, so they danced for a good hour whilst fending off eager boys. After a while they went outside for a bit of fresh air or, in Julie's case, to smoke a fag. You could smoke inside the club, but both girls were hot and sweaty from dancing and needed to cool down. The boys were getting on their nerves a bit too, as most of them were totally pissed by now and smelt of sweat and had sickly breath from too much alcohol.

'I think I'll head off after this fag, Julie. Manoli will be wondering where I am.' Scarlotte was quite drunk by now but she was one of those people who could hide it well.

'OK, duck, I'll walk back with you. My place is near to yours anyway.'

Manoli was asleep when Scarlotte arrived home. It felt funny to think that this was now home, and only a short walk from the clubs! Tiptoeing into the bathroom to clean her teeth and wash her face, she dropped her toothbrush, which made a clattering noise. Shortly afterwards, she could hear Manoli stirring in bed. Bother! I'm not going to be getting much rest now, she thought. She had hoped to sneak into bed and just sleep.

Chapter Twelve

Scarlotte woke with a killer hangover the next morning. Thankfully Manoli had toddled off to work at eight o'clock leaving her to suffer in peace. She looked in the mirror at the gruesome sight staring back at her. 'Well, don't you look mighty purty this morning,' she said to herself in her best American accent. She peered closely at her eyes which were bloodshot and had puffed up from the heat of the room. Her hair looked like she had been attacked by a large monkey in the night who had ruffled her hair into lots of big lugs. 'Lugs' was one of her favourite words and it always made her giggle because it reminded her of her mum combing her hair when she was a child. 'Hold still whilst I get these lugs out from around your neck,' Eve would say as she wrestled with the wiggly body of Scarlotte trying to get away from the painful killer comb.

She was glad that Manoli wasn't there because she had the most awful trumps. The smell was revolting, and she quickly opened the window at the side of the room whilst pulling her T-shirt top up over her nose. It must have been the gyros they had eaten on the way back last night. She could taste onions and garlic in her mouth, and felt queasy. How on earth had Manoli been able to kiss such a vile-smelling gob?

Looking around the room she discovered that her clothes from last night had been folded ever so neatly on the wooden chair next to the bed. Scarlotte had expected to see a pile of clothes thrown on the floor trailing from the bathroom. I couldn't have been that bad then, she thought as she put the kettle on for a well-needed coffee. What she didn't know was that Manoli had picked them up for her before he went to work.

Scarlotte had really enjoyed last night with Julie. She

had craved female company since coming back to Kos, and having a good chinwag with someone from her part of the world, and a boogie accompanied by some mild flirting was just what she needed. They had been chatted up so many times last night, and had she been single, she would definitely have scored - maybe even a hat-trick, she laughed to herself. Some of the guys were proper good-looking and she was proud of herself for not even snogging one of them. It took some serious willpower though! She just knew that she would become incredibly good friends with Julie and was so happy to have a female friend on the island.

Manoli had said that Scarlotte didn't need to work today. He knew that she was feeling rough and probably didn't want her moping about the shop when she should have been welcoming customers with a big smile. She was thankful for this and knew that a day lazing on the beach would be just the ticket to her recovery.

After showering, applying suntan oil and dressing in her white bikini and blue cover-up, she headed to the square for her favourite sugary pastry. Her feet were killing her from dancing last night and she found the walk of all of 100 metres a drag. The sun was hot today and was burning the parting in her hair, it must have been 80 degrees even in the shade. She must get herself a sunhat today before she got sunstroke. She quickly nipped into the nearest touristy shop and purchased a cheap white baseball cap. admiring herself in the tiny little mirror above that hat-stand. She paid the 3 drachmas for the hat, pulled the tag off and instantly felt the relief from the burning sun.

*

'Ah, agapi mou, you are alive! I like your cap.' Manoli was pleased to see his love looking almost human after leaving her looking like she'd been dragged through a bush backwards. To be fair, he had contributed to her messy hair last night which would explain the ruffled look.

'I loved it when you came home a little tipsy last night,'

he murmured. 'You were all warm and cuddly.' Obviously Manoli had ignored the fact that she did actually smell like the local kebab shop and was rather more inebriated than 'tipsy'. Scarlotte couldn't really remember much of last night but she knew that they had made love. He looked a bit tired from being woken up in the middle of the night, but he also had a twinkle in his eye so he must be feeling happy.

'How's business this morning?' she asked. 'Have you had many customers?'

'No, agapi mou, I think everyone is still in bed. We won't be busy until this evening, but I must stay here anyway, just in case.'

'I'm going to go and get myself a sunbed on the beach today if you don't mind.' Scarlotte hated asking for approval as she was used to doing what she wanted, when she wanted. He of course would be fine with that, but it didn't stop her from feeling mildly guilty for leaving him to work.

Scarlotte had told Julie that she would pop into the take-away where she worked over the next couple of days to arrange another night out. It was probably good that Julie only had one night off each week otherwise they no doubt would have been out again that night.

After settling herself on the sunbed under a parasol, Scarlotte could feel her head starting to bang as if Big Ben was chiming in her brain. Every little noise around her made her head worse and she wondered whether sitting in the sun was, in fact, a good idea. She reached into her beach bag and pulled out a strip of paracetamol, then groaned, 'Bloody hell, I've forgotten my water.'

With a great effort, she pulled on her cover-up and went to the kiosk situated next to the beach. 'Large bottle of water, please.' You could have either a frozen bottle of water, a cold one, or a warm one. Scarlotte did not like drinks to be too cold because she had quite sensitive teeth after having them whitened. 'A warm one, please.'

'There you go, darling. Warm is better for you. Ice water can give you a bad chest,' the kiosk guy explained as he stared at her boobs. Cheeky bleeder, she thought as she quickly paid the 1 drachma and scuttled back to her sunbed.

Scarlotte swigged down half of the litre bottle before making herself comfortable for the rest of the day. She'd only need to get up once to buy herself a snack later and felt pleased that she would barely have to move all day. Staring up at the clear blue sky, she watched a small plane fly overhead, pulling along a big sign to advertise Star Nightclub. Bloody hell, she so didn't need reminding of that place right now.

Scarlotte was still feeling a wee bit queasy and the thought of booze made her feel worse although it wasn't long before she drifted off into a deep sleep. She had woken herself up a couple of times by doing that pig-like snort that you did when you were just dropping off. She'd looked around embarrassed to see whether anyone had heard her. Thankfully, no one was too close to her today, so she could also let off some stinky gas from her bottom without suffocating anyone. The flies wisely also gave her a wide berth today too. God, she was a classy bird, but she didn't care today; all she wanted to do was be left alone to recover.

The local cob shop was owned by a middle-aged English lady called Jenny. Jenny had the best freshly made cobs in town. She was always pleased to see Scarlotte and they would chat about how her day had been and how lovely the weather was. Jenny always tried to get Scarlotte to have some meat on her plain salad cob, but she liked it with just a bit of mayonnaise. 'Have a bit of chicken on it, Scarlotte, or a bit of ham. You're not getting your protein, love.' Scarlotte didn't really care whether she had protein, carbs or dairy as long as she liked the taste - that was all that mattered.

At around 5 p.m. and feeling much better, with her skin

glowing from the rays of the sun and the hangover well and truly gone, she packed up her beach bag and walked along the edge of the sea. The feel of the sand between her toes and the tiny little waves lapping at her ankles was a perfect end to the day. Scarlotte still had to pinch herself sometimes to reassure herself that this wasn't a dream. Now she decided she would go home, shower and dress - and go to help her man in the shop for the evening, before they fell into bed that evening, both shattered from the previous night.

Chapter Thirteen

After their successful night out, Scarlotte and Julie made plans to go out each week on Julie's night off, and they pretty much would drink in the same places each time. Scarlotte was starting to feel a little bit bored of working in the shop, and whilst Manoli was gorgeous, he just did not have that cheeky sense of humour that she loved in a guy.

'Why don't you move in with me?' Julie had suggested. 'The rent is cheap, and you'll have more space.' Scarlotte had popped into her workplace for a chat one evening.

'I'll need to get a job though, Julie, and I don't know what I'd do.'

'Oh, come on Scarlotte, you would make a great PR! You'd easily get a job doing that and the boys definitely couldn't resist coming into a bar to have a drink with you.'

Julie was right, of course. Scarlotte never had any problem chatting with people and getting the attention of groups of guys on holiday.

'Let's ask Greg if he knows of any jobs going,' Julie managed to say through a mouthful of chips.

A week later Scarlotte was packing her rucksack ready to move in with Julie. Manoli had been mildly disappointed at her moving out but she knew they were both aware that this relationship was going nowhere fast. Besides, Manoli's friend would soon come over from Athens and move in with them, which would make the apartment even more claustrophobic, so this was the perfect excuse to announce that she was moving out.

'It's OK, agapi mou, I understand. You are young and you need to have fun.'

'It's not that, Manoli. I just think it will be too crowded when your friend comes over from Athens. There's not a great deal of room now in the apartment and I do take up all of the wardrobe space.' Scarlotte meant this but she also secretly agreed with her being 'young and wanting to have fun.'

After closing up the shop that night, they ate in the same restaurant that they had first gone to when Scarlotte arrived from England. Manoli held Scarlotte's hand over the table, just like he did on their first night together. The mood though was less exciting than the last time, and also a little awkward with tonight's topic of conversation.

'I will miss you being with me, agapi mou, but we will still be together,' Manoli said, and he smiled over the table at Scarlotte. She knew that this was not going to be the case for much longer, as she found herself quickly getting bored in his company.

*

The next day, Greg took Scarlotte to meet Ilias who owned a bar next to Poppers. Ilias had been delighted to offer her a job and she would start the following night. She would be paid ten drachmas each night and also would be able to keep any tips. As the rent was so cheap at six drachmas per night, Julie and Scarlotte would only have to pay out three each and still have some left for food and drinks; any tips would of course be spent on shoes and clothes.

This was a brand-new chapter in her adventure and now the partying would really begin.

Chapter Fourteen

Scarlotte started her new job by handing out flyers on the beach. She wore her white bikini and was slim enough to just about tie her T-shirt sleeves around her waist. She approached groups of guys and girls lazing on their sunbeds and asked them to come over to the bar that evening for a free shot with every drink. Ilias' bar was called Beaches and often just picked up custom from the overflow of customers from Poppers. It was a small bar with high round tables and stools. However, as with Poppers, most customers just wanted to stand up, dance and flirt with each other, so the tables were only used for dead empty glasses and bottles.

Ilias was around mid to late thirties and had a kind face. He had receding mousy brown hair, chocolate-brown twinkly eyes and lovely straight white teeth set in his wide face. His skin was weathered from the sun and Scarlotte thought that he was probably younger than he actually looked. Most nights he wore light-blue knee-length shorts, a bit more like 'slacks' (another word that Scarlotte liked), a baggy white T-shirt and white non-branded trainers. She wondered if he laundered his slacks each day or whether he just had a stock of the same shorts to make choosing his outfit so much easier.

He was a friendly guy though and treated Scarlotte well. He would make sure that she was not being terrorised too much by guys who were on holiday. He would stand at the door of the bar with a big smile whilst observing his empire grow as Scarlotte easily increased his custom. At the end of her shift, Ilias would give Scarlotte an extra five drachmas if it had been a particularly good night for business.

Word had gotten out that Scarlotte was a great PR and she would often be approached by other bar-owners trying to poach her for their own bar. Madness Bar was owned by

Hades, who was one of the wealthier chaps on the island. He had offered Scarlotte fifteen drachmas per night to work outside his bar. Madness was just two bars down from Greg's place, so if she moved there, then she would be able to have a laugh with Greg whilst at work. She didn't take much persuading and had softly let Ilias know the news. She felt guilty for leaving him, but she had to think of her shoe fund.

Ilias was sad to see his best PR go but a new guy had just started working for him who was really confident, so he would still have good trade and he had wished her well with her new job. She would start at Madness Bar in a week's time which would mean that Scarlotte would be able to fly back to England and attend her brother's wedding before starting her new job.

The previous night, Greg had asked Scarlotte and Julie if they wanted to spend the day on the beach with him and his friends. Greg lived in an apartment with Drake and Darren and they always spent their days on the beach. They would meet on the Friday that Scarlotte returned from the wedding, by the beach just on the edge of the main strip near to the Tropical Club. Scarlotte could not wait to get back and have some fun with those guys, especially if Darren and Drake were as cheeky as Greg.

*

The few days back in England for the wedding went incredibly fast. Scarlotte had loved seeing her mum and catching up with family members whom she had not seen for ages.

The weather had improved by then, and the day of the wedding had been warm and sunny. She was happy for her brother and his new wife, as there was nothing worse than a wedding day in the pouring rain. They seemed really great together and she was delighted to see her brother so happy. She chatted away to family and friends about her life in Greece and had a thoroughly lovely time, although she also could not wait to get back and start her new job at the Madness Bar.

The flight back to Kos proved to be a turning-point for Scarlotte: it would play a significant part in her adventure in Greece. She had chosen a window seat as usual so she could see the lights of Kos as her flight landed over the island. There was a girl sitting next to her who was going on holiday on her own to the same resort of Kardamena, where Scarlotte worked. They soon struck up a lively conversation and Scarlotte learned that Ali (short for Alison) was returning to Kos to meet up with a holiday rep with whom she'd had a fling the last time she was on holiday two months ago.

Ali was from Birmingham and had a strong Brummie accent. She had not been able to get a flight from her local airport, so her dad had driven her to Nottingham to get what seemed like the last seat available. She had a mass of shoulder-length blonde curly hair, a beautiful round face with rosy cheeks, blue eyes and plump lips which any supermodel would die for. She was much shorter than Scarlotte and had the perfect hour-glass figure.

The two girls instantly hit it off and chatted throughout most of the flight about their own lives and how they both had been on holiday with their mums and how both had been drawn back to Kos by the lure of a man. After collecting their luggage at Kos airport, Scarlotte told Ali that she must come and see her at the bar the next night. Ali agreed and promised that she would be there at 9 p.m. They would be able to catch up on the gossip of Ali meeting up with the holiday rep guy.

Ali had a transfer coach booked to her apartment and Scarlotte grabbed a taxi back to the resort. She didn't think it appropriate to ask Manoli to collect her this time since she had moved out from his apartment, although he probably would have because he was such a kind man. Julie was out at work when she arrived back to their apartment and Scarlotte was surprised to see that Julie had actually cleaned the place. Usually their room had clothes strewn all over the beds and floor, and the kitchen would have unwashed cups in it from their morning coffee together. The place smelt lovely and fresh and Julie had even washed Scarlotte's bedcovers for her. She's a good egg, she thought as she climbed between the lovely clean sheets. She didn't hear Julie come in at one o'clock in the morning as she was fast asleep within seconds of her head touching the pillow.

*

'Hey, you sleepy head, how was the wedding?' Julie leapt onto Scarlotte's bed and gave her a big hug.

'Ah Julie, it was really lovely .The bride looked beautiful, it was great to see my family and my friend Lisa. I've eaten so much food though. Do I look fat?'

Julie laughed out loud. 'Don't be stupid, there's more fat on a stick insect. Now get yourself up because we're meeting with the guys today at the beach, remember.'

They packed up their beach bags, tied their T-shirt sleeves around their middles and headed to the square to grab a coffee before meeting Greg, Darren and Drake. They passed Jenny's cob shop on the way to the beach.

'You two lovelies coming in for lunch later? Want me to make something up for you ready?' Jenny was just setting up shop and sweeping the street outside her shop.

'It's OK, Jenny, we'll just pop in later and decide then what we want if that's OK.' Scarlotte didn't like to pre-order because she had always changed her mind by the time lunchtime came.

'Don't leave it too late though because the ham sells out really quick.'

'All right, Jenny, see you later,' they both replied at the same time and giggled to each other.

'We always do that, don't we? Say the same thing at the same time.'

'Yes, we do,' they said in unison and laughed at their silly private joke.

'What are you two girls laughing at?' Greg was already face down with his chin perched on the edge of his sunbed flicking through the pages of the *Sun* newspaper. Well, not really flicking through, he was looking at the page 3 stunner of the day. You would think he would have enough to feast his eyes on with all the topless girls on the beach. Greg was a massive sun-worshipper and his skin was already deep brown despite his fair complexion.

'Nothing, Greg, we were just being silly,' Julie replied as they perched themselves on the end of his sunbed.

'I'm not paying for a sunbed, Julie. Shall we just put our towels down on the sand?'

'It's OK, girls, I've already reserved you two beds and paid for them for you.'

Greg was a real darling for doing that and they stood up at the same time to move onto their own beds.

'WAHEY!!' Greg went crash, bang, wallop over the front of the sunbed as it tipped forward with his legs in the air and his face planted down with his nose right in between the page 3 stunner's boobs.

'Ha ha ha ha! Bloody hell, Greg, you really fell for her, didn't you?' Scarlotte quick-wittedly shouted as both she and Julie erupted into uncontrollable laughter.

'Oh my God, I'm going to piss my pants.' Julie ran off into the sea to stop herself from peeing on the sunbed. Scarlotte meanwhile got up and assisted Greg back up off the sand whilst tears of laughter streamed down her face.

'I knew it was a bad idea to invite you two along,' Greg chuckled as he pulled his red swimming shorts from being wedged between his bum cheeks. They could hear Julie laughing from the sea as they sat themselves down next to each other on Greg's sunbed.

'Nearly broke my bloody neck then!'

'Oh my God, don't Greg, I'll be needing a wee in the sea

myself in a minute,' Scarlotte giggled.

Julie ran back up to them both, hopping about on the sand to avoid burning her feet, saying, 'Aargh, hot hot hot. That was bloody hilarious, Greg. Do it again for us, please.' She was still in hysterics as she grabbed her towel and dried herself off.

Drake and Darren hadn't arrived yet, they were still in bed from a late night clubbing the night before. Drake had 'pulled a cracker' apparently, Greg said, and still had the girl in his bed when Greg had left that morning for the beach. After getting over their hysterics, they all settled down for an hour's kip in the sun.

It wasn't long before Drake and Darren appeared, looking somewhat worse for wear.

'Wahey! Here's the boys!' Greg called out. 'Come on, Drake, fill us in with the gossip with the gorgeous girlie. Where was she from, what was her name, and then tell us what you did to her.' Greg always wanted to hear all the details about any encounters with female holidaymakers. He listened intently as Drake filled him in about his last night's 'bird' as he called her.

Drake and Darren were both from North Wales. This was Darren's second season in Kos, and this year he had brought along his mate Drake for the season. Drake and Darren were both of medium height and could have easily been mistaken for brothers. They both had thick dark hair, Darren's cut in a fashionable short style with a floppy fringe and Drake's a mass of neck-length curls. They were a pair of good-looking chaps and with their tanned skin and lively personalities they had no trouble pulling a new 'bird' each week.

They all sat chatting on the beach for a couple of hours and Julie took great pleasure in telling Drake and Darren the story of Greg literally falling for the Page 3 girl. They went to Jenny's shop for lunch and ate their cobs on the beach. They all got on really well and it was just as if they had known each other for years. Over the coming months a solid new friendship would blossom between the five of them, and they would create some funny memories together.

Chapter Fifteen

Scarlotte popped into the local cafe on one of the back streets, where all post would be delivered for the residents of the resort. Letters couldn't be delivered to individual apartments as there was no such thing as a postman in Kos. The main post office in Kos town would send a van into the resort each week to deliver any letters and parcels, and they would be left just inside the door of the cafe for collection. You just had to trust that no one else would pick up your letters and read your messages from home.

Scarlotte flicked through the pile of letters and was delighted to find a handwritten envelope addressed to her. She could tell that the letter was from her mum and not from Lisa as the writing was so excellently written with a fountain pen. Lisa wrote like a doctor, completely illegible. Keen to read it in peace, she went back to her apartment to sit on the balcony and open the letter before she started her shift at Madness Bar. Eve had written the letter before the wedding and it had taken a couple of weeks to arrive.

*

Dear Scarlotte

Hello, my darling, how are you? Getting nice and brown, are we?

Well, it all happens at number 10, doesn't it? Trust you to be away! It's hard to know what to write first.

Joshy is fine, you'll be glad to know. He's really streetwise now and I have a job getting him in at night. He's being mardy at the moment as I've made him stay in as I'm off to Covent Garden at 3 a.m. tomorrow (I must be mad).

Your brother's wife's parents are coming over between the 1st and 16th of August and I'll let you know the details as soon as they are definite. Robin was here last weekend, as you know. They seem really chuffed about finding out that they are having a baby. It was good for them to come here as they were sitting at home in London worrying themselves silly about money. I told them there was no way they need to worry about buying things for the baby as I've started to get some things already - well, two things to date. I bought some baby soap the first day I found out and a cute little bib this week. I thought if I buy a small item each week, I should have a nice little stash by January when the baby is due.

Can you believe that I stood in Boots the chemist for half an hour last week pricing up creams, bottles, dummies etc. I'm quite looking forward to it, but I hope they don't decide to live far away. How does it feel to be becoming a real aunty?

I'm sure if you were at home, you'd be standing beside me in Boots or Mothercare or wherever.

Actually, the news came at a good time as it takes my mind off being on my own. Saying that, Steve keeps trying to organise me into going out with him, but sitting in the pub every night isn't my scene. He made me laugh actually when he said, 'Oh, I've never dated a grandma before!' Cheeky sod.

Well, your letter and phone calls make it sound as if you're having a good time. I certainly hope it stays that way for you. I wish I could afford to come over next week but unfortunately that is out of the question at the moment.

I'm going to get my hair permed tomorrow. Linda is doing it for free for me, so I hope it turns out OK.

I'm glad to be working normal hours now that David is back off his holiday. He gave me an extra £20 yesterday for working full-time whilst he was on holiday. You know I loved looking after the flower shop on my own, but I felt so tired. It's Steve's birthday next week so the money will come in handy to buy him a present.

I've been really bored today. I was thinking about going to bingo at the local and sitting with Mrs Watts from around *the corner. If I win, then I could be over sooner rather than later!! Yay!*

Take care of yourself. Are you eating properly? I'm sure you are.

Miss you and see you soon

Love from Mum and Joshy. Joshy misses you too . . . meow!

XXXXX

*

After reading the lovely letter from her Mum, Scarlotte undressed and wrapped a towel around her ready to have a shower before work. She was just about to step into the shower when there was a knock at the door. Bloody hell, that was bad timing, she thought as she wrapped the towel tighter around her naked body and unlocked the door.

'Kalispera, how are you?' Their pervy landlord was standing at the door. His eyes wandered down to her towel-wrapped body with a sly grin on his ugly face.

'OK, thanks, just about to have a shower and go to work.'

'I just wanted to make sure there was nothing you girls needed.'

Their landlord was a fat balding middle-aged man who always smelt of body odour and had a line of sweat on his top lip. Scarlotte could feel bile rising in her throat every time she saw him. Thankfully, he left them alone most of the time, but they would occasionally catch him looking in their room as he walked past their ground-floor apartment.

'No, we're fine, thanks, there's nothing we need. Goodbye.'

Relieved that it was just a flying visit from the Fat Controller, Scarlotte quickly closed and locked the door and peeked through the spyhole to make sure that he had buggered off before she got herself into the shower. She hated it when he came around when Julie wasn't there because she felt a bit nervous about his presence. Maybe they should move somewhere else, she thought. Home should be a place to relax and unwind. Not that she needed to unwind much because she was probably the most chilled person you could ever meet, which sometimes got her into bother when trying to refuse unwanted attention. Her kind and friendly demeanour would often be mistaken for her being flirtatious.

Having dressed in her mini A-line striped skirt and black crocheted top, she left the apartment to head for work.

'Hey Scarlotte, how are you doing? Off to work?' Two girls who worked in the resort stopped to say hi. Scarlotte didn't know their names and didn't really know them, apart from seeing them around occasionally.

'Are you still seeing Manoli?' one of them asked.

'Not so much really. I don't get the time now that I'm working at Madness.'

'Oh OK, well, I just wanted to tell you that he asked me out yesterday. I said no, but I thought you should know.'

This was like a red rag to a bull. Even though Scarlotte had no intention of continuing to date Manoli, she became insanely jealous at the thought of him being with another woman, especially another English worker on the island. She could feel the burning rising up her chest as she tried to act cool in front of the girls.

'Oh OK, well, thanks for telling me. Look, I've got to get off now otherwise I'll be late.' She was sure that she heard the girls snigger as they walked off which made her even more annoyed. She marched straight over to Manoli's shop to confront him.

'Hi, agapi mou, good to see you.' Manoli was as spritely as always with a big smile on his face. However, he could instantly see that Scarlotte was not pleased to see him 'What happened?' he asked.

'I've heard you asked another girl to go out with you.'

'Well, yes, I did. I never see you, and a man has needs.'

This reply made her feel used and made her think that Manoli had only wanted one thing in their short relationship. If his needs were more important than her feelings, then this would definitely be the end of their relationship. If it still was a relationship, which it really was not, if she was honest with herself.

She stormed out of the shop, placed a fake smile on her face and went to work to deal with the rowdy drunken holidaymakers. She was not in the mood for any shit tonight. The bar was already starting to get busy when she arrived. She stopped to have a little chat with Greg on the way to work. He was always a good listener and after she'd let off some steam he comforted her, and then made her laugh - as he so easily always did. He was a really good mate and she was so happy to know him.

*

Midnight arrived quickly that night and Madness was one of those bars that did actually have soundproofing, so most of the customers made their way inside to carry on drinking and listening to loud music. Funnily enough, the bar played a lot of Madness songs which would make the crowds jump up and down, splashing their drinks all over the place. Scarlotte would try to push her way through them with a tray of drinks above her head and sometimes had to kick people's legs to get them to move out of the way. She was a good waitress though and never spilt a drink. She loved working at Madness and would always make lots of tips to top up her 15-drachma nightly wage. She would also finish work about 1 a.m., which meant that she could meet Julie from work and go clubbing.

That night after work, Julie and Scarlotte were both desperate for a wee and almost ran to the club hand-in-hand singing, 'Toilet, toilet, toilet' - and it was a good job the doorman let them in quickly otherwise there might have been a couple of very wet accidents. They always had such a laugh together. Like Greg, Julie had also become a particularly good mate and Scarlotte was so glad that their paths had crossed.

Chapter Sixteen

The next night, Scarlotte was doing her well-practised balancing act of trying to carry as many empty glasses and bottles at once back to the bar for cleaning. She was one of those people who did not like to make too many trips to achieve their objective. And here at Madness she didn't like to see empty glasses on tables; to her mind, they made the place look scruffy.

'Hiya, Scarlotte.' It was Ali, turning up a couple of nights after their chance meeting on the plane.

'Ah Ali! I thought you'd forgotten about me.' Scarlotte was really pleased to see her. 'Just let me get rid of these glasses and I will be back out. What do you want to drink?'

'Can I have a Castaway, please?'

'Good choice. Take a seat and give me two minutes.' Scarlotte hurried into the bar to drop off the glasses for the pot-washer and to fetch her new friend a drink.

Ali was looking tanned already, Scarlotte saw. She had the type of skin that only needed to glance at the sun before it went a golden-brown.

Ali thanked her for the drink and then explained that she'd not been to see Scarlotte on the first evening because she had been busy spending a night of passion with her rep guy. She had a very 'pleased with herself' grin on her face. Scarlotte had really taken to Ali: she had the same cheeky sense of humour as herself.

'So, come on then, spill the beans,' Scarlotte urged.

Ali talked through every little detail of her night with the rep. He had turned up at her apartment last night and not left until five in the morning when he had to go to the airport to transfer new holidaymakers to their apartments. Ali had been disappointed though to discover that the rep guy did now actually have a girlfriend here. She was also a rep working for the same company as him, which meant that Ali wouldn't be able to see much of him on this holiday.

'He could have told you that before you came over!'

'I would have come on holiday anyway, Scarlotte, because I just love it here on Kos.'

'OK, well, I have a fab idea. Why don't you come back and work here for the rest of the summer? You could stay with me and we'd have so much fun!'

'Oh my God, Scarlotte, that would be amazing, but I have my daughter at home. We both live with my mum and dad and I don't think I could leave her for a few months.'

But the seed was now firmly planted with Ali. All she could think about was spending a few months on this island. What an amazing opportunity it would be, and she knew she could get a job here, no problem. She would have to have a conversation with her mum and dad, though, to see what they thought. There was no need to worry about her job back home because she was a self-employed hairdresser and could easily pick up clients when she returned to England after the summer season. Her daughter Annabel was five years old and her parents had been fantastic in supporting Ali. And let's face it, she'd only be away for four months.

After a couple more days on holiday and meeting up with Scarlotte in the evenings, Ali had made up her mind. She wanted to have some fun in her life, and this was the perfect opportunity. She had phoned home to discuss it, and her mum and dad had kindly agreed to look after Annabel for the sixteen weeks that Ali would be away. They were all for her having a good break; she deserved it, they said. Ali knew that she would find it really hard to leave her daughter for the first time, but she would be able to talk with her on the phone regularly, and she was sure that the time would fly by.

In no time at all, she had secured a part-time job at a small hairdresser in Kos and was ready to return to England to sort things out with her family. Two weeks later, she would be back. And then their adventure together would begin.

*

Scarlotte had told Julie about Ali returning in a couple of weeks. Julie had already been asked by another friend if she could move into their apartment with them, but the flat was never going to be big enough for the four of them. In the end they decided that when Ali returned, Julie's friend would move into their existing apartment with her, and Scarlotte would look for somewhere else for her and Ali to live. She would start asking around today. Julie and Scarlotte would still remain good friends and meet up for drinks, and the best thing was that neither of them had any bad feelings about going their separate ways.

Chapter Seventeen

'Looks great. Can I move in from next Tuesday, please?'

Scarlotte pressed her forehead against the patio window, leaving a greasy forehead smear, to take in the lovely garden view from the apartment that she had found vacant for herself and Ali. Greg had told her about it after seeing a notice in Phil's take-away when he was buying a jacket potato last night.

The flat was directly above Phil's but situated at the back of the building, which meant that the girls would be away from the main street noise. The apartment consisted of one large bedroom with two single beds, a bathroom, a mirror above a wooden dressing table and well-placed electricity sockets which would of course be important for their hairdryers. The balcony was a decent size with two plastic chairs and a table placed on the left side, giving the best view of the stunning deep pink Bougainvillea plants growing in the grounds.

Ali would be incredibly pleased at her choice and it was cheap at 8 drachmas per night between them. The only downside was that they would only be able to live there for six weeks as the apartment had been let out after that time – but they would soon be able to find somewhere else within that time.

'When is your sexy friend Ali coming back then?' Greg asked, only half-listening for a reply as he finished reading the sport on the back page of the latest copy of the *Sun* newspaper, face down on the sunbed as always.

'Wednesday night. I'm so pleased you spotted that advert in Phil's. The apartment is perfect, and I know Ali will like it. Just one problem: we can only have it for six weeks because they've rented it out after that, so we will have to look again in the meantime. If you hear of anything,

Greg, will you let me know again?'

'Of course, darlin'.' Greg turned over to tan his already very tanned belly. He kept himself in good shape and there was not an ounce of fat on his toned abs.

'Hot today, isn't it?' Scarlotte made herself comfortable on the sunbed next to Greg, knowing he would soon be asleep after another late night with a bird. 'Pass the paper, ducky, before you nod off.'

Greg groaned at having to move from his position to reach the newspaper from under his bed. He did make her laugh; he was the life and soul of the party at night but in the day, you could get more movement out of a sloth.

'Do us a favour, darlin', and get us a bottle of water from the kiosk,' he said sleepily.

'Bloody hell, Greg, what did your last slave die of?' Scarlotte got up and took the 1 drachma coin out of Greg's oily hand. He gave her a cheeky wink and lay back down.

Scarlotte really loved hanging out with Greg on the beach. Apart from finding him hilariously funny, they were really good mates, so they would chat freely - just like he would do with any of his male friends. They didn't fancy each other so she never felt that he was coming on to her and they both had a lot of respect for each other. They were more like brother and sister.

'Oi oi! Thought we'd find you two here first.' Darren and Drake leapt onto Greg's sunbed, startling him up from his blissful thoughts of Page 3 stunners.

'Bloody hell, you gits, I was just dropping off then,' he grumbled.

'Didn't get much sleep last night, did you then? Me neither. Look, do you think you can shag a bird who doesn't snore tonight,' Darren said, and started to make snorting noises like a pig.

'Hey mate, she was bloody gorgeous though, wasn't she? She's from Australia, on holiday with her mate. They're back-packing around the world.' It was rare that you would ever hear Greg say anything bad about anyone.

'Yeah, she was all right, but I bet she's shagged a bloke in every town.' Drake couldn't help but join in on the boys' banter.

Scarlotte came back and tipped a bit of cold water from the bottle on Greg's stomach.

'Hey Scarlotte, I hear you've got a new hot bird coming to live with you?'

'Yes, Darren, and you can keep your filthy mitts off her. She's in love with a holiday rep, so you won't get a look in.'

'We'll see about that. You know she won't be able to resist my boyish good looks and irresistible charm.' He made kissing noises at her whilst framing his naughty face with his hands.

Scarlotte slapped Darren's arm and was just about to take a mouthful of her morning pastry when he grabbed it out of her hand and ran off with it down the beach.

'Oi you! Give it back!' She'd been licking her lips, looking forward to it. Scarlotte chased Darren around the sunbeds to get her breakfast back before he scoffed the lot. She was a bit lighter on her feet than him and managed to catch up with him and wrestle him onto an empty sunbed to get half of it back before he crammed the rest in his mouth.

'You're a cheeky bleeder, Darren. You wait, I'll get you back when you least expect it.'

'Mmm, that was yummy. Thanks for breakfast, Scarlotte,' he laughed whilst spitting out bits of pastry which stuck to his oiled chest.

'Roll on Wednesday when I can have some proper female company and not have to listen to you lot all day,' Scarlotte shouted as she made her way back to the others.

'Aw, come on - you love hanging out with us,' Darren said as he brushed off the crumbs from his chest straight on to Greg's legs.

'Oi, you malakas.' Greg kicked Darren's leg with his

right foot without getting up off of his sunbed. He liked to use the Greek swear-word 'malakas' as everybody knew what it meant: wanker! It was often used in jest and was not meant to be taken as an insult.

'Anyway, Scarlotte, what time is your friend coming? Want me to come with you to meet her from the airport?' Darren said, winking his eye, and nudging her arm. He'd sat himself down on her sunbed and all she could think about were his sweaty bum-cheeks making her towel damp.

'Never you mind, Darren, I am quite capable of collecting her on my own.' Actually she would have liked to have company at the airport, because she'd no doubt have a long wait for Ali to make her way through passport control, but she knew that Darren only wanted to go along to try to get 'first dibs' as he would call it, on her new friend.

The four of them spent the day on the beach chatting and taking the mickey out of each other as they always did. Scarlotte really did love spending time with these guys, they were so entertaining.

*

At four o'clock they packed up their towels and headed off to their respective apartments to get ready for work. Scarlotte wondered how the three lads managed to all get ready in the same room and whether they would fight over who had first shower. It had to be Greg, surely. He always looked so immaculate in the evenings. Darren often teased Greg for the way he carefully ironed his striped jeans. Oh, to be a fly on the wall, she thought. Then: Well, more like a mosquito in this country, she giggled to herself as she paced back to her apartment which would be home now for just the next few days.

Chapter Eighteen

Ali's flight had been delayed for an hour which meant that Scarlotte had an awfully long wait at the airport. She had managed to get off work early this evening to take a taxi up to the airport to collect her new friend. She sat outside the airport on the wall with the warm evening breeze caressing her bare arms and legs. Four other flights arrived before Ali's and the place was buzzing with new holidaymakers, reps, taxis and coach transfers.

Scarlotte searched the crowds for Ali as her flight had arrived half an hour ago; she hoped the other girl hadn't changed her mind. Then she saw her. Ali was struggling to drag her massive light grey suitcase through the arrivals' sliding doors. It didn't have wheels and kicked up a trail of dust behind it.

'Over here, Ali!' Scarlotte ran to help Ali with her luggage which must have contained her whole wardrobe because it weighed a ton! 'Bloody hell, Ali, have you got the kitchen sink in here too?'

'Ha ha ha, just about, and a lot of hair products too. Got to keep my hair in good condition in the sun.'

They embraced each other like long-lost friends, and both felt really excited to see each other again.

'Come on, let's get a taxi. We'll drop your stuff off and go for a drink before the bars close.'

'I'm starving - can we grab a gyros first?' Ali loved gyros and knew that they would be open late, just like the kebab shops in England.

'Good idea.' Scarlotte patted her tummy. 'I've always got room for a gyros.'

*

The taxi-ride to their new apartment only took ten minutes. Scarlotte had moved in the day before and had carefully unpacked her stuff, ensuring that she left half of the wardrobe and drawer space for Ali.

'I think you'll love our new place,' she said happily. 'It's got a balcony and a really fabulous view of the gardens.'

'I'm sure it's perfect, although with any luck, we won't be spending much time in there anyway,' Ali giggled as they pulled up outside Phil's jacket-potato shop.

Ali did indeed love the room and opened the balcony door to have a quick fag before they went in search of food and a drink.

'I'm so knackered, Scarlotte, but I know I won't sleep, so when I've finished this fag shall we head off out?'

'Yeah, of course. I cannot wait for you to meet the boys; you are going to love them. They're so funny, Ali, but beware of Darren because he will definitely be after you.'

'What's he like?' Ali replied as she stubbed out her fag, then wrestled in her case for her toothbrush and her make-up.

'He's good-looking, but he has been with lots of girls, that's all I'm saying.'

Scarlotte leant against the bathroom door as Ali freshened up and brushed her lovely curls.

'Right, let's hit the town! Have you warned them I'm coming?' Ali grinned as they shoved some money in their pockets and made for the door.

They bought a gyros each from the take-away place where Julie worked as they knew they would get extra chips in the kebab. However, Julie had finished for the night, so Scarlotte would introduce them another day. They took their gyros and sat on a bench in the square to eat their food.

'Still busy in the square for one o'clock in the morning, isn't it?' Ali said.

'Yeah, it's peak season now and most people don't head off to the clubs until around this time.'

Groups of tipsy girls and guys were walking through the square to head up to Stars for a night of dancing and no doubt frolicking. If they had a drachma for every time a guy asked them for a bite of their food, they would have easily been able to have a free night out on the funds. After the fifth time of being asked it got a bit boring and they made a face at each other when yet another drunken guy drooled over their food.

'Right, let's see if Greg is still at work and get a drink there,' Scarlotte suggested.

They made the short walk around the corner to Greg's place. The street was relatively quiet now due to the music being turned off and most of the customers now heading off to nightclubs.

'I think he may have finished for the night,' Scarlotte said as she couldn't see any striped trousers outside the bar. 'Let's get a drink here anyway.'

They ordered an Amstel beer each from another PR and sat on the comfy seats by the sea. They were both shattered, but it felt right to just have a drink to celebrate Ali's return. There was no way that they could have gone to a club, they were both ready for their bed.

*

The next morning Scarlotte woke before Ali. Last night Ali had pulled a nightdress out of her case before dumping it on the floor next to her bed ready to be unpacked in the morning.

Carefully opening the balcony door so as not to wake her friend, Scarlotte took a coffee out there and lit her first morning fag. She liked to have a cigarette in the morning because it would make her go for a poo before she had a shower. There was nothing worse than needing a poo when you'd just had a lovely shower and your body was clean and fresh.

'Morning, Scarlotte!' Ali shouted from her bed in her strong Brummie accent.

Scarlotte loved hearing accents from different parts of the country as this meant that she could practise copying them. With Greg being from Liverpool, Darren and Drake from Wales and now Ali from Birmingham, she would no doubt end up with an odd accent herself.

'Want a coffee, ducky?' she asked.

'Ooh yes please, and can I have two sugars?'

'*Two* sugars? Bloody hell, Ali, I don't know how you can drink it so sweet.'

'I have a massive sweet tooth. I used to have three sugars until about a month ago,' Ali confessed.

At this, Scarlotte performed a retching act as if she was going to be sick, which demonstrated her thoughts on ruining a perfectly good coffee with so much sugar. They sat outside on the balcony drinking their coffee, one extra-sweet and one with half a sugar, and both enjoying a fag together.

'So, how was your daughter when you left?' With Ali's parents looking after her little girl, Scarlotte knew that Ali might be feeling a bit sensitive about it.

'Oh, she was fine. I just told Bel that I was going on holiday but for a bit longer than normal, and that Grandma and Grandad would be looking after her until I came back. It made it easier for the both of us to look at it as an extended holiday, and these few months will fly by. I shall miss her terribly, of course.'

'Of course. But you'll be able to call and speak to her every day, which will bridge the gap. I am so happy you managed to sort everything out and come back. We're going to have a great time.'

Ali grinned and blew out smoke. 'Yes, I know. Look, I need to pop into the hair salon today to find out what days and hours they want me to work. I'll need to start to earn some money quick because I don't have that much with me.'

'Yeah sure, don't worry too much though because I have saved enough money to pay for a month's rent, so you can just pay me back whenever. We can go to the salon on the way to the beach if you like. I cannot wait for you to meet Greg, Darren and Drake. They'll probably be down there already.' Scarlotte then added, 'So, what's happening with the rep guy, Ali? Do you think you'll see him again?'

'I'm not really bothered, to be honest. As I said, he has a girlfriend now and with all of these holidaymakers readily available, I don't think I'll even notice.'

They both burst out laughing as there could not have been a truer statement.

Chapter Nineteen

The lady who owned the hairdressing salon had offered Ali work of three mornings per week to start off with. She needed to observe Ali's hairdressing skills before she would give her more hours.

'It'll do for now, but I'll probably look for something else. I don't really want to be working in the day too much as I'll miss out on valuable sunbathing time.' Getting a tan was especially important to Ali.

'Yeah, I know, but you'll be able to come down to the beach after to meet us. It's a shame though because we'll all be working at night. Perhaps we should ask around to see if there are any PR jobs going for you - what do you think?'

'Do you think I'd be able to do it? I've never done anything like that before.'

'Of course you will! If I can do it, anyone can. I used to be painfully shy when I was a child and I have managed to overcome that now. Working here has given me so much confidence, and let's face it, no one knows you haven't done it before so you can be whoever you like.'

Ali was not shy at all and she had no problem talking with people, especially guys. It was true about Scarlotte, though. She had been ridiculously shy when she was a child and would hide behind her mum's leg if anyone tried to talk to her. Hiding behind someone's leg whilst trying to get holidaymakers into a bar really was not going to work, so she had had to grow some balls and face her fears otherwise she'd have been straight on a flight back to rainy England.

'Well, hello, girls!' Greg was first on the beach again, and for once was reading a men's health magazine instead of his usual cheap newspaper.

'Morning, Greg. This is Ali. Ali, this is Greg.'

Greg got up off his sunbed and gave Ali a kiss on both cheeks.

'Be careful there, Greg, don't do yourself an injury,' Scarlotte said. 'I've never seen you move so fast.'

'Cheeky sod,' he replied as he sat back down on his sunbed just as quickly as he had got up.

Greg and Ali chatted for a while and Scarlotte could see that Ali would instantly fit into their little group. She was quick to bounce a quip back at Greg's cheeky banter which secretly amused Scarlotte. Greg had met his match with this one.

'I'll go and get us some water,' she offered. 'Do you want one, Greg?'

'No, I've got one, thanks darlin'.'

Scarlotte nipped up to the kiosk to get herself and Ali a bottle of water. She was just paying the pervy kiosk guy when she heard a roar of laughter from the beach and recognised the source of the noise as coming from Darren and Drake.

'I can see no introductions are required,' she said as she jumped off the wall back onto the beach, dropping one of the bottles of water in the sand. 'Whoops, I'll have that one, Ali. You don't want a mouthful of sand.' Scarlotte tried to brush the sand away but it was everywhere and stuck all over the wet bottle.

'Here, give us your towel, Greg.' Scarlotte grabbed the end of his towel to use it to wipe the sand off the bottle.

'Oi, get off, use your own towel. I don't want sand in my bits.' They all laughed at Greg's panic of getting even one grain of sand on his oiled body. He hated it and Scarlotte thought that he was probably in the wrong place for such a dislike of sand on his skin.

Darren and Greg chatted with Ali and made her feel really welcome. They were all good guys and if you were a fellow worker, then you would be well looked after by them.

'What's that, Drake?' Scarlotte asked. He had taken a harpoon to the beach today, apparently so he and Greg could go fishing in the sea.

'It's my tool for catching girls, what did you think it was?' Drake had a sarcastic sense of humour which Scarlotte loved.

'Oh really? I thought it was a toothpick,' she flashed back.

'We'll catch you girls some fish for dinner, or maybe an octopus if you're lucky,' Drake said.

'Don't bloody bring anything alive near me, Drake, I really have a phobia with fish,' Scarlotte said and immediately wished she hadn't. It was a big mistake to admit something like that to these lads, and she prayed that they wouldn't catch anything. Surely it would be too difficult to catch a fish on the end of this thing anyway?

'Would you cut my hair, Ali?' Greg was first to get in there on Ali's skills.

'Yeah, of course. I'll bring my scissors down to the beach tomorrow.'

'Ali, you could make some extra cash cutting workers' hair on the beach. You might not need to get another job then and you might not even need to work at the salon.' Scarlotte looked at Greg who was shaking his head as he was probably hoping to get a free haircut.

'How much do you charge at home, Ali?' she enquired.

'I usually charge eight pounds for a man's haircut but you, Greg, can have the first one free if you get me more clients.'

'Eight pounds? Bloody hell, I'll need to take a mortgage out. You might not be able to get that much from the workers here because they don't earn much money.'

'What do you think I should charge, Greg? How much do you pay now?' Ali was excited at the prospect of cutting hair on the beach, but she knew she would not be able to make as much money as she did back home in England.

'I reckon you'd have a queue of customers if you charge five drachmas.' Darren joined in the conversation as he was actually desperate for a trim too.

'OK, well, how about if I charge you guys four drachmas and anyone else five. Does that sound about right to you, Scarlotte?'

'Yeah, sounds good to me. Come on, you guys, you need to tell everyone you speak to that Ali is their new barber and she'll cut their hair wearing a bikini if they pay an extra drachma!' They all fell about laughing as Ali jokingly slapped Scarlotte's arm.

*

They spent the rest of the morning chatting before settling down on their sunbeds for a snooze. After an hour, Scarlotte went up to Jenny's shop to get them all a cob for lunch. She wrote their requests on the back of her hand and took her beach bag to carry the mass of food that the guys had ordered.

'Hiya Scarlotte, how are you today? I will be with you in a minute.' Jenny was as jolly as always to welcome her customers and there was a bit of a queue today. She was busily wrapping sandwiches and cobs in foil to take away and enjoy on the beach.

It didn't take long for Scarlotte to get to the front of the queue.

'I have a long list today, Jenny,' she said. 'The boys want loads to eat and I have a new friend here to stay for the rest of the season. I'll bring her in the next time so you can meet her - you'll love her.'

Armed with a bag full of food, Scarlotte headed back to the beach.

'Hello, gorgeous.'

Scarlotte turned around to see the blond guy from the shop opposite Manoli's. He was on his push bike and rode up next to her.

'Oh hi, how are you?' Scarlotte gave him a big smile but somehow felt a little bit awkward around him.

'I'm better now that I've seen you. I hear you and Manoli have split up. Can I take you for a drink one night?'

'Um well, I've just started seeing someone, so I can't really.' Scarlotte was crap at lying and she was also crap at saying no to people. She fumbled with her hair which was a telltale sign that she wasn't telling the truth.

'OK, gorgeous, well, you know where I am if you change your mind.' He swiftly rode off on his bike, looking back and winking at her. But she would not be going to his shop and she would not be changing her mind.

'Ugh, you'll never guess who just asked me out,' Scarlotte said to Greg as she dropped the bag of food onto his bed. Greg was too busy rustling around in the bag to pay Scarlotte much attention.

'What did you say, darlin'?' he asked as he took a big bite of his ham salad cob.

'You know that guy I told you about who has the shop opposite Manoli? He just asked me out. He gives me the creeps.'

'Well, if he hassles you, tell me and I'll have a word with him.'

That was reassuring but the guy hadn't really hassled her and Scarlotte knew she could handle him herself.

Darren and Drake had gone into the sea to try to catch their dinner on the end of their toothpick. They took it in turns to dive below the surface of the water and aim the arrow at anything that moved on the seabed. Then they would return to the surface coughing and spluttering and without a fish in sight.

'Bloody idiots. Why bother with that malarkey when you can get a good fish meal down at the Adelphia restaurant.' Greg had no time for such activity and would rather be served food already cooked on a plate.

'We should all go there one night,' Scarlotte said as she

looked at Ali for approval.

'Sounds good to me. Do they do swordfish? It's the only fish I'll eat.' Ali had acquired a taste for the meaty flesh of swordfish the last time she was in Kos, but any other type of fish made her nauseous.

'Yeah, of course they do, darlin'. Let's arrange a date when the guys are back from messing about in the water.' Greg almost knew the menu there off by heart.

The three of them demolished their cobs whilst watching Darren and Drake continue their quest to catch supper. After about an hour the two boys swam to shore and jogged back up to their friends.

Drake sat next to Scarlotte on her sunbed.

'Hey, get your wet arse off my bed.' She smacked Drake on his back as he flicked freezing cold seawater on her belly, then let out a loud scream of terror as Drake held a little dead fish in front of her nose. Scarlotte leapt off the sunbed and ran down the beach with Drake hot on her heels. When he caught up with her, she grabbed Drake's arm as he tried to shove the dead fish in her face. He hadn't realised just how petrified Scarlotte was of fish until he saw the tears running down her face and the blood dripping down his arm from her nails digging into his skin.

'OK, OK, OK, I'll throw it away.' Drake chucked the fish across the sand and feeling very guilty, he helped Scarlotte back to her sunbed. Her heart was beating very fast and she started to feel a bit sick from the fright.

'You've gone a bit pale, mate, are you all right?' Ali made Scarlotte sit down next to her on her sunbed and put an arm around her trembling shoulder.

'Oh my God, Ali, I'm so sorry. I didn't realise your phobia was that bad.' Drake felt devastated that his joke had gone so horribly wrong. His arm was red and bleeding so he used the serviette from his cob to stem the drips of blood.

'It's all right, Drake, you didn't mean any harm,' Scarlotte told him shakily. She knew he'd just been mucking around. 'It's just I have had this fear since I was about five years old when I stood on a fish with my bare feet in a neighbour's garden.'

Of course, everyone thought this was hilarious. There was a moment of silence and then they all cracked up, with Scarlotte releasing her tears as laughter instead of fear.

After the fish drama it was time for everyone to go back to their apartments and get ready for work that evening. Ali would stay on the beach for another hour or so and meet them later in the evening.

Chapter Twenty

Ali was a couple of years older than Scarlotte. She had trained to be a hairdresser when she was pregnant with her daughter. This had allowed her to choose the hours that she worked, fitting them around ante-natal classes and visits to the hospital. She had gone home to live with her mum and dad, ever since she had split up with the baby's father. She never really spoke about him because as far as she was concerned, he did not exist any more. He had cheated on her two months before the birth of their child. At the time she had been devastated and heartbroken - but knew that she had to be strong for the child growing inside her.

The first couple of years of being a single parent had been tough and she often wondered how single mums coped if they lived alone with their baby. She was so lucky to have supportive parents and knew that she would have struggled without them. While she lived at home, she could still go out with friends, carry on with her job and not allow her life to change too much with this perfect little bundle to care for. She loved Annabel with all of her heart and wished her daughter could have had a father. Despite herself she sometimes wondered if the relationship with her ex could have worked out if she hadn't found out about his infidelity.

For the first three years after giving birth, Ali had gone on holiday with her parents and her new baby. However, when the little girl was old enough to be looked after by just her dad and the rest of the family, she had started to have a week's holiday away each year with just her mum. This year was the second time that Ali had been to Kos with her mum, and at that time she would never have thought it possible to move here without her daughter - until she met Scarlotte.

Ali really liked Scarlotte. The moment they had started

chatting on the plane, she knew that they would become good friends. Their conversation had flowed freely and there were no awkward silences. Little had she suspected at the time that a couple of weeks later she would be moving to Kos to share an apartment with this new friend. Nor had she suspected that she would fall in and out of love so many times on the island of Kos, and finally recover from her heartbreak.

*

'This swordfish is amazing.' Ali cut herself another slice of the delicious fish and popped it in her mouth. Adelphia really was the best restaurant in town and the five of them had reserved a table for half past four to allow them time to enjoy a meal together before work.

Greg was making everyone laugh as usual as he pushed two olives on sticks into the top of his cob which made very odd-looking eyes – then he made it talk like Zippy from the kids' TV programme *Rainbow*. He was a nutcase and amused them all so much.

Scarlotte had ordered liver and onions. Drake had told her that it was the best in town, and he was not wrong. The liver was so tender that it melted in your mouth, and the onions had been cooked in butter and were browned on the edges to give them the most delicious smokey taste. The meal of course came with the obligatory mound of chips.

Drake polished off his food first as he needed to get to his job. He was working in a of Chinese restaurant just on the edge of town. It was one of the busiest restaurants in Kardamena, which surprised Scarlotte as she could never understand why British people went to Greece and didn't eat the local cuisine. It didn't make sense to eat food that you would have as a Friday-night take-away back at home, when you could try anything from freshly made Greek salads to delicious homemade moussaka and mouthwatering desserts like melomakarona – made of honey, oranges, oil and nuts. Oh well, each to their own, she thought.

Drake dropped his 5 drachmas on the table and gave the girls a peck on the cheek before he toddled off to wash dirty plates for the night.

'Hey Ali, I was talking to the guys who work on the watersports in front of Poppers this afternoon. They're all up for a haircut when you're available.' Greg was pleased with himself for drumming up some business for Ali.

'She's always available for hunky watersports guys,' Scarlotte quipped with a mouthful of chips.

'Ha, Scarlotte, funny girl. That's great, Greg, thank you. I'll go over there tomorrow with my scissors.'

'I might have to come with you to make sure they form an orderly queue,' Scarlotte said and winked at Ali.

After thoroughly enjoying their meal, Greg, Darren and Scarlotte needed to get to work.

'You coming with me to have a drink at Madness?' Scarlotte asked Ali.

'Yes, of course. I might have a wander around the shops first, so I'll catch up with you later.'

Darren had gone off ahead of them to start his work as a PR at another of the bars at the end of the front strip. He started his shift half an hour earlier than Greg and Ali. The bar he worked in, which was called B52, was tailored more to couples who were having an early drink before their meal, so it was a bit different to the rowdy groups of youngsters that frequented Greg and Scarlotte's bars. Darren had worked at B52 since the beginning of the season and he liked that he would finish at midnight when their music was turned off. He always made lots of tips too as couples tended to tip more than the younger holidaymakers who were often on a budget.

'I might try to get a job in a quieter bar. I could do with earning some extra money in tips and it would be great to finish a bit earlier,' Scarlotte said to Greg as they walked through the square to work.

'It wouldn't suit me. I much prefer to be chatting to the young dolly birds than serving couples a pre-dinner drink. I don't think I'd be able to score as much.' Greg nudged Scarlotte, nearly knocking her over.

'You are just terrible, Greg! I can't fault you though,' she told him fondly, nudging him back and making him almost trip over a stray cat strolling casually to the nearest restaurant to seduce the holidaymakers into thinking it was starving. 'Poor little pussy cat,' the ladies would say as they passed scraps of food under their tables before the waiters shooed the hungry felines away.

That night at work, Scarlotte carried on thinking about changing her job to a more relaxed environment. Working at Madness was fun, but she had started to get tired of dealing with drunken groups of guys and girls. She would start her quest tomorrow to seek a new job.

Chapter Twenty-one

'Morning, Scarlotte.' Ali was awake first this morning and already sitting on the balcony drinking her coffee and having a fag. The smell of cigarette smoke had wafted into the room and up into Scarlotte's nostrils, waking her up. The net curtain covering the window had started to acquire a lovely tinge of yellow from the smoke.

'Want another coffee?' Scarlotte dragged herself out of bed and put the kettle on.

'No, I'm OK, thanks. I've just made this one.'

They hadn't gone out clubbing yet since Ali had come back, and despite planning to go last night, they were just whacked after eating the big meal at Adelphia.

'Hey, Ali,' Scarlotte shouted from the kitchen. 'Do you fancy coming with me so I can ask around the bars on the back streets today to see if they need any PRs? You could ask too.'

'What was that?' Ali bawled. She couldn't hear from the balcony, especially with the kettle hissing and just about to come to the boil.

'Hang on a sec.' Scarlotte made her milky coffee and carried it outside, where she sat down on the plastic chair next to Ali.

Then: 'Ouch! That's bloody hot. It's nearly taken the skin off the back of my legs.' She jumped up off the chair and put a tea towel on it before sitting back down as Ali sniggered. 'I said, do you fancy having a walk along the back streets today to see if any of the bars need a PR?'

'Yes, if you like. I might ask around too. I'd love it if we could both get a new job near each other.' Whilst Ali had some snipping and clipping to do on the beach, she wouldn't really make enough money to keep her going. The hairdressing salon only paid her a pittance and Scarlotte thought that they were taking advantage of Ali. Working at the salon also ate into her sunbathing time which was already getting on Ali's nerves.

'Darren was telling me that he earns about ten drachmas in tips each night at his bar,' Scarlotte said. 'It would be great if we both could earn extra cash and then we could buy some new clothes - and shoes, of course.'

'Yes, because you *definitely* need more shoes,' Ali replied cheekily.

Scarlotte looked at her reprovingly. 'A girl can never have too many shoes, Ali. Surely you know that?'

After showering they headed off to seek out new jobs. The first couple of bars didn't have any vacancies, but the guy who owned the second place had pointed them in the direction of a bar called Cafe Marina. Apparently, they needed a PR to help to boost their business.

Cafe Marina was owned by an elderly Greek couple and run by their son Nico. Nico was still in bed when they arrived at the bar and the owner, who didn't speak too much English, asked them to come back in the afternoon when his son would be there. Disappointed, the girls walked back through the square, passing Manoli's shop. He was inside putting T-shirts on the shelves, so they quickened their pace so he wouldn't see them pass. Just after Manoli's shop on the left was a relaxed bar called Sunshine, where they could see the middle-aged owner carefully placing his new cushions onto the wicker chairs at the front. His wife was busy cleaning the inside ready for another day of business.

'This looks like a lovely place, Scarlotte. Shall we go in and ask?'

'Looks a bit too quiet for me, Ali, but fill your boots.'

Ali strode ahead with a big smile on her face to chat to the owners while Scarlotte remained outside, looking back to see if she could spot Manoli, but he was still inside. Bored of waiting for what seemed like ages, she took a walk down the street to have a browse in the shops. There was a new shop selling Levi jeans which looked interesting.

'Kalimera,' the owner said as she approached. 'Come in and take a look, please.'

'Yassou. Thanks.' Scarlotte flashed him her best smile and entered the little shop. There were all colours of jeans in different styles and she could do with a new pair. 'How much are these, please?' She picked up a pair of dark blue skinny jeans. They didn't feel too thick, so she wondered if they were fake.

'For you, my love, they are ten drachmas.'

Must be fake at that price, she thought. She picked up another lighter blue stone-washed pair and was pleased to hear that they were also only 10 drachmas.

'Oh, I like them both, but I don't know which ones to have. What do you think?' she asked the owner. Not that he would know which ones were best for her, as he was not exactly a style guru himself in his white socks and brown sandals.

'My darling, take them both. You can have them for ten drachmas but don't tell everyone, please.'

'Wow, really? Are you sure? That's fantastic, thank you.'

Leaving the shop with her two new pairs of jeans in a white carrier bag, she could see Ali walking confidently towards her with a spring in her step and a happy expression on her face.

'I can't leave you for five minutes, can I, without you buying something,' she said as she stuck her nose in Scarlotte's carrier bag.

'Never mind my shopping - they're jeans, by the way. What did they say?'

'I got a job!' Ali jumped up and down, grabbed Scarlotte by the arms and danced around the street. 'Can you believe it! They're such a lovely couple and they've not been open long, so they've been thinking about getting a PR to help start their business up.'

'Wow, Ali, that's bloody amazing! When do you start?'

'Tonight at eight p.m. and they will pay me twelve drachmas per night rising to fifteen if I get lots of customers for them.'

'Oh my God, I'm so pleased for you, ducky.' They both squealed with delight, much to the annoyance of an elderly British couple passing them in the street.

'Let's go back to the apartment so we can drop off these jeans, fetch our beach towels and go and tell the boys,' Scarlotte suggested. 'Oh, and if we can pop in that other bar on the way back out, I can see if Nico is there.'

But Nico still wasn't there when they went back to the bar, so Scarlotte decided to try again later.

'Guess who's got a job, boys?' Ali ran to their friends on the beach, clapping her hands together in an excited fashion just like Annabel would do.

'Ah, well done, mate.' Darren and Drake both got up off their sunbeds to give Ali a kiss on her cheek, while Greg just beckoned her over for a kiss, so he didn't have to move his body.

Ali told them about the new bar called Sunshine and how the couple who owned it were really lovely. Scarlotte felt so happy for her new friend and knew that she was going to be a fantastic PR for them.

'I guess you won't be going over to the watersports today then to cut their hair?' Greg said, pointing at his own head and hinting that he actually needed his hair cutting.

'No, I can't be bothered today now I've got my new job to think about. They will just have to wait.' Ali tossed her head as she proudly emphasised the last sentence.

*

On their way to work that night, Ali and Scarlotte made the slight detour to Cafe Marina. Both of them were looking their best. Scarlotte was wearing her new light blue jeans which fitted her slim figure like a glove.

Cafe Marina was on the second street back from the

main street. It had football shirts hung all around the bar, a large TV on the wall at the back for football games to be shown and a DJ booth at the rear on the right, which would play the latest pop and garage tunes until midnight. The bar would attract couples in the daytime and early evening, so they could sit outside with a cocktail or a coffee. Whilst at night the bar would be livelier, with younger groups of guys and girls. It was a good mix of customers.

'Hi, are you Nico?' Scarlotte had waited for the loud Greek guy to finish chatting and joking with a couple of English holidaymakers about the football league.

'Yes, darling. How can I help you? I think I've seen you around - don't you work here?' Nico had a quizzical look on his face as he wondered if he had in fact seen Scarlotte before.

'Yes, I work over at Madness, but someone told me that you might be looking for a PR here.'

'Yes, I am, darling. Do you want to come and work here?' Nico said as he lit a cigarette. Scarlotte couldn't help but notice that his eyes kept wandering across to Ali who was leaning over the bar with her ample breasts almost falling out of her top.

Nico was a giggly and larger-than-life fella whose laugh could be heard from about a mile away. He had a typical Greek nose, dark, slicked-back hair, alert brown eyes and slightly crooked teeth. He was a tall guy with a large build and a bit of a beer belly. However, he was very charming in a way, and Scarlotte could imagine that his cheeky personality would make him very fanciable to the ladies. He was around six foot and wore a trendy crisp white polo T-shirt with jeans. He also smelt amazing, of a spicy aftershave.

'When would you like to start here?' he then asked her. 'I can pay you fifteen drachmas each night. We are getting really busy now and I could do with someone to PR but also serve drinks to the tables. Does that sound OK to you?'

'It sounds fantastic! When can I start?'

Scarlotte would start work there the following night which meant that she could tell Madness Bar that tonight would be her last night working there.

'See you later, darling.' Nico said goodbye and waved as they left the bar with his eyes following Ali's every move.

'I think you've pulled there,' Scarlotte told her.

Ali wrinkled her nose. 'He's not really my type, is he?'

'I don't know, mate, but I think you're definitely *his* type!'

They skipped off, both feeling very happy with themselves. Tonight would be Ali's first night in her new job and Scarlotte would start her new job tomorrow. Today had been a highly successful day for them both.

Chapter Twenty-two

Ali's first night in her new job had been uneventful but she had enjoyed it, nonetheless. The bar was still relatively quiet and those customers who did come in were mostly couples enjoying their pre-dinner drink. She had spent a lot of the night talking with the owner and discussing ways in which they could get more customers. Ali had suggested that they make some flyers and she would give them out on the beach and also that they could possibly play more up-to-date music. Their music choice was OK, but they didn't play the latest tunes from the charts. The owners didn't really want to attract too many groups of girls and guys to the bar as it was more of a relaxing place to have a drink than a crazy beach-front bar. The good side to this though was that Ali would finish early each night at twelve o'clock when the bar closed; also, the probability of getting a tip was higher.

'What did they say at Madness when you told them that you were leaving?' Ali lit a cigarette and offered one to Scarlotte as they strolled to find breakfast the following morning.

'They were fine. You know Paris who manages the bar for Hades? Well, he said that I can go back there if I don't like it at Cafe Marina.'

'That was kind of him. Isn't he the good-looking one?'

'Yes, Ali, he's the one we definitely both wouldn't mind shagging.'

Paris was very handsome, and all the girls fancied him. He was very cool and trendy and had the looks of a movie star. He was about the same height as Scarlotte, had dark hair with a floppy fringe hanging in curtains over his gorgeous, unusual hazel eyes, and a smile to mesmerise any unsuspecting female. Both Ali and Scarlotte would flirt unashamedly in his company.

'I fancy a Full English Breakfast this morning, what d'you reckon?' suggested Ali.

'Oh yeah, that would just hit the spot. The restaurant next to the kiosk on the beach does English breakfasts. Shall we go there? We can then just flop straight onto the beach.'

'You mean waddle onto the beach after eating a mountain of food!'

They both rubbed their bellies and pushed them out as far as they would go, making themselves look pregnant.

Greg was early on the beach today. The girls invited him to join them, but he did not want to 'ruin his figure' by filling his body with a greasy fry-up.

'A moment on the lips, ladies,' he shouted as they made their way up to the restaurant. 'A lifetime on the hips!'

The breakfast was really tasty, and the restaurant served proper English sausages, not those horrible frankfurter ones you'd get in most places abroad. They also had brown sauce which was like gold dust in the resort.

'Bloody lovely, that was,' Scarlotte said whilst wiping her plate with toast to get the last bit of runny egg. Ali attempted a reply but it came out as a big burp instead.

'Ali, you dirty bleeder, you're such a lady. Not.' Fortunately no one had heard her belch and the girls fell about.

'Oh my God, you do make me laugh. Shall we go and have a kip on the beach?' Scarlotte paid the waiter out of their kitty which they had made up to make it easier than trying to split the bill each time they ate - which was most of the time.

They plodded down to the sunbeds and settled down next to Greg.

'Look at the bellies on you two. I wouldn't make a habit of eating a greasy breakfast every day,' Greg commented as they got themselves comfy.

'Hark at you, Mr Universe,' Scarlotte replied as she slapped Greg's tummy.

'Hey ladies, you won't find an ounce of fat on me.' Greg tensed his abs so you could see his six-pack.

'More like a two-pack, that, Greg,' Ali chirped up from her sunbed with one eye open, making them all laugh.

'Ah, this is the life, hey?' Scarlotte lay down feeling very content with her friends by her side and the sun blazing down on her skin. This really was magical.

*

'Oi oi, make room for the good-looking ones.' Darren and Drake materialised just after noon. They perched themselves on the sand at the bottom of the sunbeds.

'Nice of you two to join us. These two fat ladies have only had a Full English this morning, greedy blighters.' Greg wasn't going to let up on their choice of food that morning.

'Ah man, I could murder a breakfast right now,' Darren groaned.

'I think they do them all day - why don't you both have one? It'll keep you going for the rest of the day.' This was something that Scarlotte's mum would say to her when she made a lovely big breakfast.

The two guys trotted off to find a table and order themselves an all-day brekkie.

'I'm sweating here in the sun, it's so bloody hot today.' Ali sat up as the sweat from her neck ran down her chest onto her boobs. 'I'm going to sit on the wall for a bit in the shade.' She took her towel and placed it on the concrete area at the edge of the beach, where she was mostly shaded by two large motorbikes that had been parked there by two guys having lunch at the restaurant.

Greg and Scarlotte lay peacefully in the sunshine until they were woken by a scream.

'OW! HELP! HELP ME, PLEASE, SOMEONE!!'

Scarlotte knew instantly that it was Ali. She and Greg

leapt off their sunbeds and ran towards their friend, who was flapping her arms and legs about under one of the motorbikes that had fallen on top of her.

'Bloody hell, Ali.' Greg had managed to heave the heavy bike off of Ali with the assistance of its owner, a big burly German guy. Scarlotte meanwhile helped Ali up into a sitting position.

'The handlebar fell straight on to my chest,' Ali whimpered. A bruise was already starting to appear on top of her chest, just below her right collarbone.

'Do you need to go to hospital?' Scarlotte was really worried about her friend.

'No, no, I'm OK, honestly. Just help me up back onto my sunbed and I'll be fine.'

Greg and Scarlotte assisted Ali to the safety of her sunbed so she could lie down. Darren had dashed off to get her a bottle of water and Drake was shouting at the German guy for leaving his bike in an unsafe position.

'Bloody rude he was,' Drake swore. He rejoined them after having had a row with the motorbike owner, who had called Ali a 'silly English Girl' - even though Ali had not even touched his bike. 'I was going to punch the bloke, but he was the size of a house.'

Ali and Scarlotte looked at each other and grinned at the image of Drake trying to wrestle with a six-foot German mountain of a man.

'Ah bless you, Drake, thank you,' said Ali, who was still very shaken up and in pain. 'And thank you to you guys for rescuing me.'

'You gave us all a fright there, Ali. I thought I was going to have to take you to the hospital. An inch higher and it would have broken your collarbone. Are you sure you're all right?' Scarlotte was sitting with her arm around her best mate.

'Yes, honestly I am. I'll just lie down here and recover from my shock.' Ali put her arm up to her forehead and performed a fake fainting, which made them all laugh, but mostly it was the laughter of relief.

Chapter Twenty-three

It was Scarlotte's first night at her new job in Cafe Marina. She felt a bit nervous as she would be the only PR working there. Whilst she had grown in confidence, she still felt a little self-conscious about dancing around outside a bar whilst trying to entice strangers to come in and have a drink. Some of the PRs on the island had no such inhibitions and did not care two hoots what people thought of them. Scarlotte was a little more sensitive and would take it to heart if anyone said anything negative about her.

Nico wasn't around when she arrived promptly at 7 p.m. The barman was there, however, and he was expecting her.

'Hi, I'm Leo.' He held out his hand.

Scarlotte shook Leo's hand.

Leo had a native American-Indian look about him with long brown hair tied in a ponytail at the back of his neck. His skin was a lovely olive colour, his eyes were very dark brown - almost black - and he had a very slim face and body. He was not what Scarlotte and Ali would call good-looking, but she was sure that he would be very attractive to some girls.

'Nico will be here about eight p.m.,' Leo said now. 'He told me to get you a drink - what would you like?'

Scarlotte leaned over the bar to look in the fridge which held a vast array of alcoholic drinks.

'I don't know what I fancy, what do you suggest?'

'I will make you one of my very special cocktails.' Leo busied himself mixing it for Scarlotte as she sat on the wooden stool by the bar. There were only two couples in the place at this time and the music was playing gently in the background.

One couple got up from their comfy seats outside and thanked Leo as they left. Scarlotte quickly whipped into action and collected the empty glasses off the table.

'Where's the cleaning stuff, Leo, oh and the ashtrays?' She wandered behind the bar in search of a cloth to wipe the table. She had taken the full ashtray already and emptied it into the bin. Leo showed her where everything was, and she meticulously cleaned the now empty glass table.

'Crikey, those tables only usually get a quick flick of the cleaning cloth. I can see that Nico's parents are going to love you.' Leo placed a large cocktail glass on the bar, the sort you would usually get a Pina Colada in. The liquid inside the glass was thick like a Mr Whippy ice cream and looked more like a milkshake than a cocktail.

'Wow, that looks yummy, Leo - what is it?'

'For you, my darling, on your first night I thought I would treat you to an Orgasm.'

'Ha ha ha, very funny. What's in it?'

'Bailey's, Kahlua, Amaretto and ice cream. Try it, you will like it.'

Scarlotte took a cautious sip with the straw. 'OH MY GOD! That is gorgeous! Definitely the best orgasm I've had in a long time.' Scarlotte took another sip of the lovely creamy coffee-flavoured ice-cream drink.

Leo laughed at her quip. 'You see? You came to work in the right place!'

A few more customers stopped by for a quick drink before their evening meal and Scarlotte served them at their tables. The first couple left her a two-drachmas tip for her trouble, and Scarlotte had a feeling that this was going to be a really good job.

'Hello, darlin'.' Nico's entrance could only be described as a tornado whipping around the bar. He was such a large character and the atmosphere in the bar was instantly lifted to another level 'Fucking hell, you on the cocktails already?' he joked to Scarlotte as he put out his cigarette in an ashtray behind the bar.

'Yes. Leo made it for me. Thank you for the drink, by the way.'

'My pleasure, darlin'. Wow, have you been cleaning? The place looks spotless. There's usually glasses all over the shop when I get here.' Nico nodded in approval. Scarlotte felt happy that Nico had noticed her hard work already. She did have a strong work ethic and always liked to make a good impression on her boss.

'Just needed a woman's touch,' she said, and winked and clicked her tongue.

It was just after 8 p.m. and the streets were starting to get busy with a younger crowd of holidaymakers. Nico had turned up the music and Scarlotte stood outside ready to terrorise people into coming into the bar. The DJ wouldn't arrive for another hour, so Nico had recorded some cassette tapes with the latest tunes which he played from a sound system behind the bar.

As Scarlotte boogied outside to the latest chart tunes like 2 Unlimited's 'No Limit' and Shaggy's 'Oh Carolina', she pulled in groups of girls and guys to enjoy an Orgasm in the bar. This would be her hook to get them into the bar, she had decided. 'Fancy coming in for an orgasm, boys?' always did the trick.

Leo was sweating behind the bar; he had never made so many Orgasms in one night. The bar was so busy that Nico had had to help out with serving the drinks. Scarlotte was running backwards and forwards to serve customers who had sat outside on the comfy seats, and as quickly as a customer left their table, it was filled again with more. The DJ had played some awesome tunes which had made it much easier to feel confident jigging about and Scarlotte had made herself at least 15 drachmas in tips on her first night, which was the same as her nightly pay. She was extremely happy.

The last of the customers left around 1a.m. Scarlotte helped Nico and Leo bring in the tables and chairs from outside and clean the bar. It didn't take long and they were finished for 1.30 a.m.

'Thank you, my darlin', you have done amazing tonight.'

Nico handed Scarlotte her pay for the evening and she stuffed it into her jeans pocket.

Scarlotte left the bar with a big smile on her face and felt so excited to have found such a great place to work. She and Ali had arranged that whoever finished work first would go and meet the other one at their bar. Scarlotte was surprised that Ali hadn't already come to her at Cafe Marina as Sunshine Bar tended to close a bit earlier.

All of the gift shops that lined the road to Sunshine were now closed, so there was no chance of her bumping into Manoli. The square was busy though, as always at this time of the night, with people making their way to one of the nightclubs. As Scarlotte passed the square she could see Ali outside Sunshine talking to a middle-aged couple who looked like they were the last customers in the bar.

'I wish they'd go home; they've been sitting outside on their own for an hour now,' Ali whispered as they both walked inside the bar.

The owner was at the back counting his takings for the evening; his wife had already gone off to bed.

'A good night then?' Scarlotte asked the owner. She still did not know his name.

'Yes, it has been really busy thanks to Ali.'

Ali smirked at Scarlotte as she started to move some of the cushions off the outside chairs which would hopefully give the last customers the hint that they wanted to close. Scarlotte gave her a hand and it wasn't long before the last customers bade them goodnight.

'Leave the cleaning tonight, Ali, I'll do it in the morning.' Her boss was a lovely guy and he could see that Ali was desperate to go off with her mate and he also wanted to get home to his wife.

'Are you sure? I don't mind doing it now.' Ali felt obliged to offer, although she could tell that Scarlotte was desperate to get away.

'No, honestly Ali, you get off.' Her boss shut the till and

got his keys ready to lock up.

'You nutcase, we could have been there another hour cleaning up,' Scarlotte whispered to Ali as they walked away from the bar.

'Just trying to make a good impression.' Ali did the most massive yawn. 'Anyway, how was your first night in Cafe Marina?'

'I love it there.' Scarlotte dipped into her jeans pocket and showed Ali the tips that she had made that night.

'Bloody hell, mate, that's brilliant. I think I made about eight drachmas tonight.'

'Hey, I'm impressed - that's almost a new pair of shoes.' Scarlotte always had shoes on her mind.

The original plan was to meet up after work and go to a club, but they were both knackered tonight from working hard in their respective bars.

'Shall we just go to bed tonight? I'm so tired.' Ali yawned again.

The friends linked arms and headed back to their apartment where they fell into bed and were soon sound asleep, feeling happy but exhausted from a busy night's work.

Chapter Twenty-four

As the girls got themselves ready for another day on the beach, Ali mentioned that the guys working at the watersports had popped into her bar last night to ask if she would cut their hair.

'Do you mind if we go down there first so I can sort them out before we meet the boys?' she asked.

'Of course I don't mind,' Scarlotte replied, swearing as she struggled to get one of her feet into its very unruly flipflop.

'You all right there?' Ali grinned as Scarlotte kicked her flipflop across the room.

'Bloody things. Think I'll put my wedges on instead. At least they don't give you sore places in between your toes. I can just take them off when we get to the beach.'

After buying a coffee from the square, the girls strolled down to the seafront. The watersports area was situated directly in front of the main square, about 200 metres from the beach that they usually frequented. This beach was always packed with holidaymakers and the sunbeds were crammed too close together for Scarlotte's liking. The sunbeds cost more money too, as you were close to all the bars and restaurants.

'Where's my coffee?' Danny, who was the manager of the watersports team, was sitting under his wooden hut in the shade. His team were out on the water bouncing some poor girls over the waves on a large inflatable banana, before tipping them off into the deep sea. Scarlotte and Ali watched the girls struggle to pull themselves back on the banana before the speedboat whipped them around and tipped them off again.

'It looks like fun but you wouldn't get me on that thing,' Ali said. She wasn't keen on getting her hair wet, so a ride on this particular type of banana wasn't going to be on her bucket list.

'Why don't you two girls take a pedalo out when you've cut my hair? You can have one for free but don't go out too far because it's windy and you'll end up in Turkey.' Danny moved his plastic chair out of the hut and onto the sand.

'Oooh yeah, shall we, Ali? You can pedal and I'll just sunbathe.'

'Erm, I don't think so. You're fitter than me, so you can do the pedalling,' Ali replied.

Danny really fancied himself and Scarlotte found him rather arrogant. He was just a bit too cocksure - which was probably brought on by girls throwing themselves at him because he worked on the watersports. He was just under six feet tall, had short spiked fair hair, blue eyes and a toned body. At about thirty years of age, Danny was a bit older than the other guys working on the watersports, but no doubt the boss needed to have a few more years of experience behind him, Scarlotte thought.

Ali started snipping away at Danny's hair while Scarlotte sat on the sand next to them.

'Bloody hell, Ali, I'm getting covered in hair here,' she grumbled. It was quite windy as Danny had said, and Scarlotte appeared to have sat on the wrong side of his chair, resulting in the wind blowing tiny specks of blond hair all over her.

'Move then, you silly sausage,' Ali replied as she combed the top of Danny's hair and placed it expertly between her fingers before snipping it off.

Danny was impressed with his haircut and admired himself in the tiny mirror that they kept in their hut. Of course, the guys would need to regularly check themselves in the mirror to ensure that they looked good.

Not quite David Hasselhoff though, are you, ducky? Scarlotte thought to herself.

Ali was expecting to cut all of the watersports guys' hair

whilst she was there, but they were particularly busy that day taking people out onto the sea.

'Tell them I'll come back in a day or so to do their hair, Danny,' Ali said. She didn't mind. She and Scarlotte were keen to get out on a pedalo and have some fun.

Danny pulled the last available pedalo into the sea and helped them climb aboard.

'I reckon this is the old jalopy of the pedalos,' Scarlotte commented as they started to move the rusty pedals up and down with their feet. 'No wonder it was the last one left on the beach.'

The pedals squeaked as the craft spun around, and it took some real leg power to loosen them up enough to get some movement out of the floating rust bucket. The sea was quite choppy with the wind blowing so hard. The girls pedalled and steered the best that they could to keep close to the beach edge and both quickly got a sweat on.

'We seem to just be drifting further out, Ali.' Scarlotte looked at her friend, who was now resting her legs on the front of the pedalo to get maximum sun exposure. 'Oi, get your lazy feet back on those pedals and help me to try to get us back closer to the shore.'

They both started to pedal as hard as they could, but the sea just kept carrying them further and further away from the shore. They were starting to feel a bit anxious by now, especially as their arm-waving to get attention from the shore went unseen. Luckily, a guy on a jet-ski passed them and noticed that they seemed in distress. Well, mildly distressed as they were pissing themselves laughing too.

'Are you OK?' the guy shouted from his jet-ski.

'No, we can't get back in. Would you tell the guys on the watersports for us, please?'

The guy sped off to shore to seek help for the girls.

Drifting further out to sea, Ali and Scarlotte did genuinely feel a bit scared now. The sea was quite rough further out, and it looked really deep now below them.

'For fuck's sake, what did I tell you!' Danny was looking none too pleased as he pulled up next to them in the speedboat. Ali and Scarlotte pretended to be remorseful as he helped them off the pedalo onto the boat. 'I'll have to bloody tow it back now. Why didn't you stay close to the beach like I told you to?'

They felt like they were getting told off by their dad which made them giggle even more.

Danny attached a rope to the pedalo and started to slowly tow it back to shore with the girls safely onboard the boat.

'Danny! Danny - I think it's sinking!' Ali shouted over to Danny who was looking ahead in the direction of the beach.

Scarlotte bit her lip as she watched the pedalo start to take on more water.

'Oh Jesus Christ, this is *so not* what I need today.' Danny was getting truly ratty by now and was regretting letting the girls take the pedalo out. He stopped the boat and stormed to the back to see what was happening. Then, going back to the steering wheel, he moved the boat really slowly to try to prevent the pedalo from taking on any more water.

'Oh dear.' Ali put her hand to her mouth as the pedalo slowly sank into the sea. Bubbles surrounded the little craft as pockets of air made their way to the surface. Ali looked at Scarlotte who had her head in her hands to stop Danny from seeing her laughing.

Fortunately, they were now close enough to the shore for the pedalo to be rescued by the rest of the watersports team. They dragged it slowly out of the sea and tipped it upside down to remove the remaining seawater.

'We're so sorry, Danny. We tried really hard to stay close to the shore, but the wind and the tide just took us further out.' Ali had to apologise because Scarlotte was still on the verge of hysterics, partly from knowing what danger they had been in and partly from the way they'd been told off; she knew she would burst out laughing if she tried to talk. Ducking away, as usual in these situations she avoided all eye contact with Ali - because if they caught a glimpse of each other she wouldn't be able to control herself.

'I shouldn't have let you go out really,' Danny said gruffly. 'It's OK, girls, it's my fault.' He seemed to have calmed down a bit, now that the pedalo and the girls were safely back on the beach. After Ali had promised to go back the next day to cut the rest of the guys' hair, the two girls scuttled off giggling.

It was later in the day than they had expected so they decided to give the other beach a miss. The sea air had made them both very hungry and they fancied a proper meal before going to work later that evening. After polishing off a good plate of beef stifado and roast potatoes they went back to their apartment for a little kip before another night in their new jobs. What an eventful day it had been for the both of them and definitely not one that they would ever forget – or would like to repeat!

Chapter Twenty-five

'That stifado is really repeating on me,' Ali said as she did a loud belch, mouthed 'whoops' and put a hand over her mouth a few seconds too late. She was on the balcony smoking a fag and Scarlotte had just had a lovely hot shower and was drying her hair.

'Make sure you dry your hair underneath today,' Ali said bossily. 'You always leave it damp and it goes all knotty around your neck.'

'Yes, mistress.' Scarlotte looked heavenwards. Ali constantly nagged her about not drying her hair properly and, as Ali was the expert on hair, Scarlotte would follow her instructions.

Following a little kip after their pedalo fiasco and large meal, the girls were feeling refreshed and ready for anything.

'Shall we go to Tropical Club tonight after work?' Scarlotte shouted over the hum of the hairdryer.

'Yes - isn't it tonight that the boys said that they were going? I think they want to watch the wet T-shirt competition.'

'Oh God yeah, I forgot about that. Maybe you could join in, Ali?'

'No bloody chance,' her friend said firmly. 'The only place I'll get my boobs out is on the beach and definitely NOT on a stage in a nightclub.'

After doing their make-up they left their apartment to go to work.

'Try to get off early tonight so we can get to Tropical at a decent time,' Ali said and gave Scarlotte a hug. They waved to each other as they went their separate ways.

*

Cafe Marina was already quite busy tonight with a group

of football fans watching an old England game on video. Thankfully, the game only had ten minutes to go as Scarlotte really was not a football fan. There were empty bottles and pint glasses everywhere and Scarlotte could see that Leo the waiter was rushed off his feet.

'Crikey, Leo, looks like you've been crazy busy!' Scarlotte immediately started to collect the dead glasses and place the empty bottles in the large plastic glass bin behind the bar.

'Can we get some more drinks over here, darling?' a guy who sounded like a Londoner shouted over to Scarlotte.

'Yes, sure. What can I get you?'

'Five pints of Amstel, please - ooh and a date with you, sweet'eart!' The cheeky guy gave her a wink as he turned his attention back to the game. His mates were too engrossed in the match to notice the tall blonde waitress who was there to serve them.

Scarlotte fetched the drinks from the bar and carried them over to the group of lads. Just as she was placing them down on the table the lads let out a loud roar as England scored in the final minutes. She almost jumped out of her skin!

'You nearly wore that pint then,' she laughed at the guy who'd ordered them as she managed to save the last glass which was now wobbling precariously on the edge of her tray.

'You can pour a pint all over me anytime, darling,' he said, winking at her as his mates now joined in on the banter.

'I wouldn't touch him with a bargepole, love. You dunno where he's been,' called one.

'Yeah, but we *do* know where he's been, and you really need to keep your distance otherwise he'll 'ave you up them apple and pears before you know it,' another guy piped up.

The lively lads were from south-east London, or 'sarf-east Lahndan' as they pronounced it.

Scarlotte liked their accent and she listened carefully to enable her to improve on this particular accent. Fortunately, the guys didn't stay long after their last pint and wobbled off to get ready for a night out in the resort.

'I bet they'll be terrorising a few girls tonight,' Scarlotte said to Leo as she collected their empty glasses.

'Yes, if they don't all crash out after a skinful of beer,' he laughed.

There were only a handful of people left in the bar when the whirlwind that was Nico arrived.

'Hi Scarlotte, hi Leo. How are you both tonight?' Nico was as bubbly and full of beans as usual as he turned off the TV and put a music cassette tape on.

'It's been busy with a group of guys from London watching the England match video.'

'Facking 'ell, that's good innit?' Nico replied in his best London accent, then laughing at himself.

Scarlotte really liked Nico; he was very funny and could copy any accent from the UK with great accuracy. Customers would love to hear the larger-than-life crazy Greek bar-owner take the mickey out of them by answering them in their own regional accent.

'Hey Scarlotte, how is your friend Ali?' he asked now.

'She's getting on fine, thanks. She's working at Sunshine now.'

'Oh yes, that new bar on the opposite side of the square. Can I ask you something? Does she have a boyfriend?'

'No, she doesn't at the moment, but perhaps you should ask her?' Scarlotte couldn't lie to her boss but she wasn't sure if Ali would mind if she had told Nico that she was single.

'Yeah, I might pop down there now and say hello before we get busy.' Nico picked up his packet of cigarettes off the bar and headed towards Sunshine Bar.

Scarlotte had no means of warning Ali that Nico was on his way, but she knew that Ali could handle herself and would be capable of giving as good as she got from Nico.

Nico returned after half an hour with a massive smile on his face. 'She's fucking mental, your friend,' he grinned, pointing to his head as he strode into the bar.

'What did she say?'

'She's meeting me tomorrow afternoon for coffee.'

She *must* be mental to miss out on several hours of sunbathing, Scarlotte thought to herself and now could not wait to finish work that night to get all of the gossip off Ali. Especially since Ali had said that he wasn't really her type.

Nico was particularly loud and boisterous tonight and Scarlotte could see that he was excited at having a date with Ali, even if it was just coffee.

*

The streets were not that busy tonight as it was changeover night, which meant that a lot of holidaymakers went home, and new arrivals would be in the resort for tomorrow morning.

There were a few couples sitting outside the bar enjoying a drink whilst people-watching and one lone guy had been sitting at the bar for an hour now. Scarlotte felt a bit creeped out every time she had to pass him, because he would stare at her and his blank facial expression never seemed to change. He was a tall, slim guy with dark cropped hair, and a thin face with piercing dark eyes. He wore faded blue jeans, a green and white striped short-sleeved shirt and brown loafers.

Scarlotte had attempted a friendly smile at him a couple of times but he just stared back at her. Trying to ignore the strange man she nipped off to the toilet which was just at the end of the bar under the TV. Sitting down to have a wee with her elbows on her thighs and chin resting on her hands, she shut her eyes for a couple of minutes. She felt tired tonight and was waiting to get her second wind. Not the type of wind that came out of your bottom, the type of wind which gave you more energy.

Pulling up her knickers, something made her look up at the grate which was high up on the wall in between the men's and ladies' toilets. She felt a burn of heat run through her body as she saw two steely dark eyes staring down at her.

'What do you think you're doing?' Scarlotte shouted as she quickly made herself decent, opened the toilet door and ran out to Nico.

'What's wrong, darlin'?' Nico could see that she was distressed so he took her into the back and put his arm around her.

'That, that man who was sitting at the bar - he was spying on me through the grate in the toilet.' Scarlotte was close to tears now with the shock of seeing those scary eyes perving down at her.

'What the fuck? Really? Right - let me deal with him.'

The man was already back on his seat at the bar when Scarlotte and Nico approached him.

'Hey mate, my friend tells me you were looking at her in the toilet. What do you think you're doing?' Nico was calm and professional when he spoke to the man but could quite easily have lost his temper if the fellow hadn't just got up and walked out without saying a word.

Nico followed him out of the bar and watched the man walk away down the street. 'Don't worry, Scarlotte, he has gone. If you see him again, you tell me - OK?'

'Thanks, Nico. He gave me a fright, that's all. I'm all right now.'

Leo made Scarlotte her favourite Orgasm cocktail which would make her feel much better and Nico had given her permission to finish a bit earlier so she could go to meet Ali. He hoped that Scarlotte would tell Ali what a kind boss he had been to her tonight which would put him in good stead for a romance with her.

*

'Hark at you dumping me tomorrow daytime to go and

have a date with Nico,' Scarlotte teased Ali as she was getting her purse from behind the bar in Sunshine.

'Ha ha ha, very funny, I'm only going for a coffee with him.'

'Yes, but we all know what *coffee* means, don't we, eh?' Scarlotte winked at her best friend.

'No, I don't think I fancy him, but he seems like a good laugh, doesn't he?' And Scarlotte nodded in agreement.

On their way to Tropical, Scarlotte filled Ali in on the dirty pervert who was spying on her in the toilets. 'I feel a bit anxious in case we see him,' she said, 'so make sure you don't leave me alone at all tonight.'

Ali had been shocked at this news and promised to 'kick him in the balls' if she saw him. She performed her best high-kick and arm-chop, shouting, 'Hi yah!' in a Miss Piggy voice from *The Muppet Show* which made them both crack up. Scarlotte loved that her mate could instantly cheer her up and make her forget such a horrible incident.

Tropical was already busy with holidaymakers having a good time. The place wasn't even half the size of the Stars nightclub, which meant that it seemed even more packed. The same number of people in Stars would only fill about a third of the place. There were three bars - one on the left-hand side of the dancefloor, one at the far end of the club and one upstairs. The latter had a balcony which allowed customers to watch people below.

The DJ announced that the wet T-shirt competition would start in half an hour which resulted in a loud cheer from the dancefloor. Ali and Scarlotte went in search of the boys and found them at the back of the club chatting to a couple of Greek guys.

'Hey boys, get 'em in,' Scarlotte said as they nestled their way into the little group. Greg ordered them both a Blastaway, which would get them in the mood for dancing.

'Thanks, Greg,' they both said, taking a big swig of the fruity alcoholic drink.

'Come on, girls, let's get to the front so we can see the wet T-shirt competition,' the three boys said, so they obediently scuttled behind them.

There were five girls taking part in the competition and each in turn would have a little interview with the host before a bucket of water was thrown at them.

'Classy birds!' Ali shouted in Scarlotte's ear as a large-breasted girl lifted up her T-shirt to show all and sundry her ample bosoms. The boys in the crowd cheered and wolf-whistled, which egged all five of the entrants to do the same when their turn came around.

Scarlotte and Ali left the boys to it and went back upstairs to get another drink. The first-floor area was busy with guys looking over the balcony at the show and girls milling around, sipping their fancy cocktails whilst waiting for the male attention to turn back on to them.

Ali ordered them both a bottle of Amstel lager which they drank straight from the bottle. The barman also gave them a shot each of some blue-looking liquid which tasted like pure sugar.

'Urgh, that was disgusting.' Scarlotte pulled her sour lemon face as she knocked it back in one go. Ali loved it because it was sweet and ordered two more.

'Don't make me drink another one, please!' Scarlotte made Ali drink them both as she ordered herself a B52 which was a shot of carefully poured layers of Baileys Irish Cream, Kahlua and Grand Marnier.

They were both feeling quite tipsy now because of course they had already been drinking at work. The boys joined them and spent the next couple of hours dancing and checking out the latest female talent in the club. Every two weeks there would be a new batch of holidaymakers arriving which resulted in the boys having a new conquest each time there was a changeover.

Ali was dancing with Darren in a dirty dancing fashion. Both were very drunk and ended up snogging on the dancefloor. Scarlotte and Greg were standing by the bar at the side of the dancefloor watching them with amusement.

'I bet they end up shagging,' Greg shouted over the music.

'Wouldn't surprise me, but Ali mentioned that she was feeling a bit sick earlier, so I'm not sure it would be a good idea.' They looked at each other and laughed.

As if on cue . . . 'I think I'm going to be sick!' Ali cried as she ran past them with Darren hot on her heels.

'What's up with Ali?' Drake literally put down the girl he had been swinging around the dancefloor and did a silly dance as he approached Scarlotte and Greg.

'She's just feeling a bit queasy from mixing her drinks. Darren's gone in the Ladies with her anyway, so he'll look after her.'

'Yeah - I bet he'll look after her good and proper,' Greg said, nudging Scarlotte's arm which made her laugh. She knew that Ali was safe with Darren, so she didn't want to go in and overcrowd her. The toilets were not very big and two people in there would already be somewhat 'cosy'.

Around fifteen minutes later, Ali and Darren emerged from the toilets giggling to each other.

'Were you sick?' Scarlotte asked.

'Yeah - just a little bit though. Darren held my hair back for me while I boffed up those blue shots.'

'Mmm, Good work, Darren.' Scarlotte patted him on the back for taking care of her friend.

'I think it's time to head off now.' Greg was yawning which set Scarlotte and Ali off yawning too.

They all left the club together in desperate need of some food to soak up the alcohol. It was 4 a.m. now though and hardly anywhere was open. There was a soup kitchen near to the Star nightclub, but they couldn't be bothered to walk there so they made do with the gyros van which was parked outside Tropical.

Eating as they walked, they went along the front strip

and parked themselves on a wall by the sea. The boys finished their food first and headed off home, leaving Scarlotte and Ali lying down on the wall, head to head with knees bent, looking up at the night sky.

'Come on then, Ali, spill the beans. What happened in the toilets with Darren?'

'Oh my God, can you believe that as soon as I'd stopped being sick, we had sex?'

'No bloody way! Did you still have your head hanging over the toilet?'

'Yes. I don't think he wanted to kiss a sickly mouth.' Which made them both snigger.

'It's getting light already.' Scarlotte yawned and closed her eyes.

'Shall we just sleep on one of the sunbeds on the beach?' Ali suggested, half-joking.

'Come on then. I can't see anyone around so we shouldn't get into trouble.'

They jumped down off the wall and climbed onto two plastic sunbeds. The cushions were always put away at night by the owners. Ali squeaked about on the plastic as she tried to get comfortable whilst Scarlotte just lay on her back, feeling a little bit nippy with the sea breeze.

At exactly the same time, they looked at each other and said, 'Shall we go?'

They both got up quickly, jumped back over the wall and headed to the square where their apartment would have two comfy, proper beds waiting for them.

Chapter Twenty-six

The landlord of Scarlotte and Ali's apartment dropped a real bombshell on them the following morning. At 9 a.m. he banged on the door and woke them. He'd come to inform the girls that he needed them to move out within two days. The people who were renting the room from him had moved their dates forward, so he needed to clean the place ready for their arrival.

'Bloody hell, Ali, that's a pain in the arse,' Scarlotte grumbled as she and Ali went out onto their balcony for a cigarette, feeling much the worse for wear. 'It means that today will have to be spent looking for somewhere to live.'

'Oh God, but I've got a massive hangover from last night and I'm supposed to be meeting Nico too.' Ali took a couple of paracetamols with her coffee and put on her darkest wide-rimmed sunglasses.

'Probably a good idea not to spend the day on the beach then. There is nothing worse than the sun blazing down on you when you feel rough. Let me get you some water.' Scarlotte went to the fridge, got out a large bottle of water and filled two glasses.

'Let's have a shower to try to liven ourselves up a bit and then go and get some breakfast,' she told Ali, passing her a glass. 'That'll make us both feel slightly more human again. We can pop into Cafe Marina and tell Nico that you can't make your date with him today if he's there. If not, we'll just leave a message with his dad.' Scarlotte was also feeling under the weather, but she was the type of person who preferred to suffer in silence. She did not like people to make a fuss of her if she was feeling unwell.

After an hour of grunting from Ali as she got ready, they made their way towards the square. They popped into a few shops to ask the owners if they knew of any rooms to rent but to no avail and they left a message with Nico's dad. After eating an FEB in the restaurant by the beach, they continued their quest.

'I know - let's ask Danny on the watersports if he knows of any rooms available,' Ali suggested. 'He's worked here for years so I bet he knows everyone in Kardamena.'

'Good idea, but you can ask him because I don't really like him.' Scarlotte still blamed Danny for the episode with the pedalo. It could have ended with them drowning, if the craft had sunk with the two of them still in it. The pedalo simply hadn't been seaworthy, and yet he'd tried to stick the blame on them at first.

Scarlotte waited on the same wall that they had been lying on just a few hours earlier, whilst Ali strutted ahead to talk to Danny. He was sitting in his little hut as usual with his feet up and hands behind his head.

Scarlotte could see Ali chatting and laughing with Danny and she wondered what they were laughing about. Come on, she thought. Stop flirting, we've got a room to find. After another five minutes she became impatient and joined them in the hut.

'Hi, Danny,' she said, and managed to bring herself to smile at him. 'Do you know of any rooms then?'

'Yes, I was just telling Ali that there's a couple of guys who I know are going back to the UK tomorrow and they have an apartment up near Stars nightclub. If you wait until my guys bring in the speedboat, I'll walk you up there. It's only five minutes away.'

'Oh great. Thanks, Danny.' Scarlotte felt a bit bad for saying she didn't like him, now that he was going out of his way to help them. She still thought he was arrogant though.

As soon as the other watersports guys came in from the water, Danny was true to his word. He put one of the team in charge so he could nip off with the girls. Also, he was proved right: the apartment was only a five-minute walk and it was set back from the main road on the way to Stars. They turned off the road onto a dusty path which led to a large white apartment block. The two young men were packing in their first-floor apartment when they arrived.

'Hi mates, have you found someone to take over this place yet?' Danny shook each of their hands.

'No, buddy. Are you girls interested? You're welcome to take it over. We've paid until the end of the month, so if you could pay us for the next week's rent, then you won't need to pay anything until the first of next month,' one of the guys said turning to the two girls. Apparently, they had to rush off back to the UK to sort out their university placements and their flight was booked for the following morning.

'What do you think, girls? Do you have the money to pay these fellas today? If so, I guess you can move in tomorrow then if the landlord is cool with that.'

The apartment was huge. It had two bedrooms and a massive balcony. They all went downstairs together to find the landlord to confirm that the girls would be taking over the rent from the first of the next month.

It all sounded more than reasonable and Scarlotte handed over a week's rent, trusting that all would now be in order.

The following day, Scarlotte packed her rucksack and Ali packed her large grey case ready to move out. Their current landlord apologised for the inconvenience of asking them to move out with so little notice, and thanked them for their efforts in finding a new place so quickly.

The walk up to their new place made them sweat. It was a hot morning and Ali's suitcase was a real pain to drag along the dusty roads. 'You need to get a case with wheels, ducky. That's like humping around a big elephant.' Scarlotte tried to help but it was difficult with her own heavy rucksack on her back.

Their new landlord was waiting for them outside the

building when they arrived. 'Kalimera,' he said. 'Welcome to your new home. Can I take your rent please for the rest of this month?'

Scarlotte and Ali looked at each other, confused. 'We paid the tenants that were here before us. They told us that they'd already settled up with you until the end of the month.' Scarlotte felt a rush of concern as she dropped her rucksack on the floor.

'No, my darling. They did not pay me. You have to pay now before you can move in.'

'I can't believe this!' Ali puffed as she balanced her bum on her suitcase, wiping the sweat off her brow.

'We're going to have to pay again, Ali. We've got just about enough money to cover it, I think.'

They couldn't very well argue with the man. The flat was too lovely to risk losing. The girls got out their purses and having reluctantly satisfied the landlord's request, they were taken to the first-floor apartment and provided with the key. Feeling really annoyed that these boys had ripped them off (or was it the landlord?), they dropped off their bags and headed to the watersports to see if Danny had seen the lads around.

Danny was out on the speedboat when they got there, so they wouldn't be able to speak to him. To be honest, there wasn't anything he or they could do about it now anyway. The girls agreed that they would just have to learn not to be so trusting in future and focus on earning lots of tips over the next few nights to make up for their loss.

The good news was that they now had somewhere to live, and while the rent was the same as their last place, the new apartment was much bigger, meaning that they could have a bedroom each. With mixed emotions of annoyance and happiness they decided that they might just as well forget about it now and enjoy the rest of their day. After popping back to their new place to get changed into their bikinis, they headed for a well-required kip on the beach.

Chapter Twenty-seven

'Wow, look at all of this room! We can do our own washing and hang our knickers out without anyone seeing them.' Scarlotte was excited. She and Ali were having a proper look around their new home, which had been cleaned ready for them. The balcony had a long washing-line tied diagonally from one corner to the other, which was a bit dodgy, as they would have to be careful not to decapitate themselves.

'You'll have to be careful your knickers don't get k-nicked,' Ali said with a straight face. 'You can see them from a mile away they're that big!'

'Ha - you can talk.' They laughed at each other's cheek - so to speak.

They had recovered from their trauma of being ripped off yesterday and both had sensibly had an early night after work. 'Early' meaning before 2 a.m., and they hadn't gone to a club.

'I'm surprised we couldn't hear people come out of Star last night,' Scarlotte said as she leant over the balcony and observed just how close the club was to their apartment.

'You were out flat last night, and you did that scary thing where you sleep with your eyes open.' Ali had often had conversations with Scarlotte across the room whilst they were in their beds, sharing a room, not realising that her friend was, in fact, fast asleep.

'I don't do that,' Scarlotte argued. 'Stop taking the piss! How can anyone sleep with their eyes open?'

'Well, you bloody do. I have to turn over because I can't look at you. It's frankly creepy.'

'Really?' Scarlotte made a face. 'Honestly, I didn't know that I did that. Though my mum said I used to sleepwalk a lot when I was a child. I don't do that as well, do I?'

'Oh God, don't tell me that! Next thing, you'll be walking around the apartment with your eyes open and be fast asleep at the same time. It'll be like living with a flipping zombie. Now that really would freak me out.'

'You wouldn't complain if I sleepwalked and did the washing for us though, would you? Or if I did the ironing?' Scarlotte thought about it. 'Imagine if I could do all of the chores in my sleep and wake up to find them already done.'

'I wish,' Ali replied. 'I'd sneakily leave all of my ironing on your pile, so that you did mine too.'

'I'd know they were yours, even if I was asleep, and I'd throw them at you.' Scarlotte grabbed a T-shirt and threw it at Ali's head.

'Right, stop mucking about now and let's get ready and get ourselves down to the beach,' Ali said, then fled as Scarlotte chased her around the balcony with a pair of knickers in her hand.

*

Greg, Darren and Drake were already at the beach when they arrived.

'Crikey! Couldn't you sleep?' Scarlotte said as she and Ali plonked themselves on the end of Greg and Darren's sunbeds.

'Just maximising the sun today, ladies,' Greg said without moving an inch as usual.

'Hi, Darren.' Scarlotte winked at him and raised her eyebrows. 'I hear you looked after Ali good and proper the other night in the club,' with emphasis on the 'good and proper'.

'You can rely on me,' Darren replied as he clicked his tongue and adjusted the back of his shorts whilst lifting his bum off the sunbed.

'Hey, there's a workers' party outside Poppers Bar tomorrow daytime,' Drake piped up. 'Are we going?'

Greg grunted from his sunbed, 'Ugh, no thanks, I never go to those. They're just full of people getting drunk and then going off and shagging each other.'

'How very shocking.' Ali gave Scarlotte a knowing look. They would definitely be going.

'What about you two?' Scarlotte asked Darren and Drake.

'Yeah, of course we'll be there. We'll leave Grumpy on the beach with his page three busty lady in the paper.' Drake splashed Greg with his bottle of water.

'Oi, you. I'm not grumpy, I'm just choosy about who I socialise with.' This was true. Despite being the most confident PR in the resort, Greg saved his personal time for just a few close-knit friends.

'Hey, Ali, shall we go in the sea for a swim?' It was another hot day and Scarlotte could feel her skin burning.

'Yes, but I don't want to get my hair wet. Shall we buy those Lilos we looked at the other day?'

'Oh my God, that's a brilliant idea. We can get the ones with the windows in the pillow so we can look through them at the seabed.' Ali and Scarlotte had longed to buy these Lilos but their last apartment didn't have the room to store them without having to deflate them each time they took the Lilos home.

Leaving the boys to sunbathe and ogle the girls on the beach, they trotted off to a shop near to the square to buy their new toys. Ali chose a pink one and Scarlotte a yellow one. The shop-owner kindly inflated their Lilos for them, so they were ready to go. Although it was a really hot day, it was quite windy which made carrying the Lilos a precarious task. They had to struggle to control their inflatable toys. A gust of wind caught them as they passed a street opening to the sea. Ali's Lilo flew out of her grip into the air and whacked an old Greek man on the head; he had been quietly sipping a coffee on his doorstep. His coffee cup went flying and he almost fell off his little wooden stool.

'I'm so sorry!' Ali ran after her Lilo in her flipflop-laden

147

feet. Dust was flying everywhere from the gust of wind and from the back of her flipflops. Scarlotte was standing cross-legged trying not to wet herself and holding on extra-tight to her own Lilo. For Ali, saving her precious new inflatable was obviously more important than checking that the old fella was OK. She'd just spent her hard-earned cash on the Lilo, and an old bloke's spilt coffee wasn't going to get in the way of the rescue mission.

Thankfully the Lilo had got wedged between two postcard stands at a shop just down the road, allowing Ali to recover it without the need of further flipflop sprinting. Crying with laughter, Scarlotte sat on a nearby wall to stop the wee from coming out of her body. She could just about see Ali through the tears of laughter in her eyes. She saw her go back to apologise and see if the old man was all right before she sheepishly walked back to Scarlotte.

'Oh my God! Can you please do that again? That's the funniest thing I've seen in a long time.' Scarlotte got up and continued the walk back to the beach with Ali, adding, 'What did the old man say to you?'

'He was fine,' Ali giggled. 'He just said something in Greek. He was smiling so I guess he wasn't too angry with me.'

'Oh, it was so funny.' Scarlotte was still wiping the tears of laughter from her cheeks. 'Wait until the boys hear about this one.'

They both continued to giggle at each other all the way back to the beach. When Ali told the story of her unruly Lilo nearly taking the old man's head off, the boys cracked up. Ali would never be allowed to forget this incident, and it would definitely be brought up in future conversations.

After they had all recovered, Scarlotte and Ali gripped tightly onto their Lilos and tiptoed into the sea.

'Oooh oooh oooh, aaah aaah aaah, it's freezing!' The sea was just at the top of Scarlotte's thighs and going further in would mean freezing off her lady bits. 'I'm going to try to get on here,' she shivered.

Ali was already floating around face-down on her Lilo. 'Watch out!' she cried, 'There's a fish!' She pointed to where Scarlotte was standing. The freezing cold water was now no challenge for Scarlotte as she launched herself on her Lilo with such speed that she slipped straight off the other side. Coughing and spluttering, she bobbed up from the water underneath the Lilo, sending it flying in Ali's direction, shouting, 'Quick, grab it!'

Ali reached out with her right arm and caught the Lilo before also sliding off her own and ending up under the sea. She popped up, spluttering and sweeping her curly blonde locks out of her face.

Scarlotte was pissing herself again and this time there was no need for leg-crossing as she was in the sea - she would just make that bit of the water a bit warmer.

'Oh nooo! I'm going to have to wash my hair tonight,' Ali complained as she mounted her pink Lilo again.

'That was an amazing catch, Ali,' Scarlotte thanked her as she struggled onto her saved Lilo and attempted to get herself face down in the same position as Ali.

The girls floated towards each other and linked fingers to keep themselves together as they looked through their pillows, which made their Lilos like little glass-bottomed boats.

'Look, little fishies!' Ali was first to spot a shoal of tiny little fish swimming around the shoreline.

'Aw, they're so cute.' Anything larger than a tiddler then Scarlotte would have been front-crawling her way to the shore.

They spent the next hour bobbing around on their Lilos and trying to master the art of turning over without slipping off. By the end of their session they could confidently manoeuvre their bodies without even getting wet.

'Ah, that was fun,' they said in unison as they placed their Lilos next to the boys who were chatting away about some girls they had met the previous night.

'Don't take up sailing,' Greg teased them as they used their towels to dry themselves off before lying down on their trusty Lilos in the sun to get warmed up.

'Oi, watch it, you,' Scarlotte said. 'We are now fully qualified competent Lilo sailors, I'll have you know.'

'I hate having wet pants,' Ali said as she wiggled around on her squeaky Lilo.

'Not what you said the other night,' Darren quickly quipped, before turning back to the other boys to continue their chat.

'Hey Drake, what time does the workers' party start tomorrow?' Scarlotte asked.

'Around twelve noon, I think. Shall we see you there?'

Scarlotte looked at Ali for approval and she nodded in agreement. 'Sounds good to us.' Neither of them had been to a workers' party before and they were looking forward to it.

After hanging out with the boys on the beach, they walked back up the hill to their new apartment near Star. It was about four o'clock now and the wind had dropped slightly, meaning that it wasn't such a challenge to carry their Lilos.

As they neared their apartment, they could see a man walking ahead of them. He was about 100 metres away so they couldn't tell if they knew him - he looked like a Greek man though with his dark hair. He was obviously walking faster than them as the gap between them grew. They noticed that he kicked something off the road into the bushes.

'What was that?' Scarlotte looked at Ali as they quickened their pace to see what it was that the man had kicked. As they approached the bushes, they could hear little cries of distress.

'Oh my God, look!' Scarlotte leaned into the bush to see four tiny little kittens huddled in a ball. Her heart felt like it was going to explode as she carefully lifted the kittens one by one and passed them to Ali. They were little tortoiseshell furballs with their eyes only just starting to open.

'Aw, they are so cute! I could murder that man for treating them like that.' Scarlotte was fiercely protective over animals and would seriously consider clouting anyone who would cause harm to a defenceless creature.

They looked around the area to see if they could locate the kittens' mother cat, but she was nowhere to be seen.

'Let's take them into town to see if anyone knows of a cat who has recently had kittens,' Scarlotte said as she snuggled two of the babies up on her chest.

Thankfully, none of the kittens appeared to have been harmed and they seemed happy to be cuddled with such genuine love for them. Ali nipped up to their room and dropped off their Lilos whilst Scarlotte sat on the ground and attempted to hold all four of the kittens. She was actually in heaven and wished that she could keep them - she would have a houseful of kittens if she had her own way.

They walked into town, carefully holding the babies who were making the most heart-wrenching little meow noises. They asked in a couple of shops in the square and were told by a Greek girl that one of the places on the front had a resident cat, and that she was sure that it was heavily pregnant. With the kittens held close to their chests they found the restaurant at the far end of the front strip.

'Excuse me,' Scarlotte asked a Greek lady who was just inside the doorway preparing vine leaves for the evening menu. The lady looked up and raised her arms in joy. She dropped the vine leaves on the table. 'Come,' she said, and quickly guided them to the back of the restaurant. They entered the back garden of the building to see a large tortoiseshell cat curled up in a corner looking extremely sad.

'Oh my God, I think that's their mummy.' Scarlotte

walked towards the large cat and carefully held one of the kittens near to her. The cat seemed to spring to life. She got up and started to lick the kitten. Scarlotte and Ali placed the remaining kittens with their mother. Scarlotte had tears in her eyes from this wonderful sight and she felt so happy to have reunited the babies with their mother.

'Thank you, thank you, thank you,' the Greek lady said as she cupped first Scarlotte's, then Ali's face in her hands.

'You are welcome,' Scarlotte replied as they reluctantly left the joyous scene to head home to get ready for work.

'How amazing that we found their mummy. I don't know what would have happened to them if we hadn't found them in the bushes - and what would we have done with them?' Scarlotte was beaming from ear to ear.

'I know you, Scarlotte, you'd have smuggled them into our apartment,' Ali said affectionately. She was equally happy at their amazingly good deed for the day.

Chapter Twenty-eight

Ali didn't have to be at work until an hour after Scarlotte that evening so she decided to have a drink in Cafe Marina before she started. Secretly she wanted to see Nico and have a good flirt with him whilst Scarlotte started her work. The bar was already quite busy this evening so Leo the barman and Scarlotte were kept busy serving drinks and chatting with the customers.

Ali sat herself down at the end of the bar closest to the front of the street which would give her full view of anyone passing by. Tonight, she had made an extra effort to look her best. She was wearing her short white denim skirt with the buttons down the front, a fitted blue low-neck T-shirt which showed off her best assets, and her hair was freshly washed with the curls flowing down her back. Her make-up was perfect, and she had even applied her gorgeous pink lipstick.

'You're on a mission tonight, aren't you?' Scarlotte whispered in her friend's ear as she hurried by to serve a couple who were reading the cocktail menu outside.

Ali winked at her friend and took a big swig of her blue cocktail made extra-strong by Leo the barman. As if on cue, Nico burst into the bar literally a minute later.

'Fucking 'ell!' he exclaimed as he went straight to Ali and wrapped his arms around her. 'Where have you been? I've missed you.'

Nico was obsessed with Ali and this would be the perfect start to an evening for him. He pulled up a stool next to her and offered her a cigarette whilst Leo was instructed to get them both a fresh drink. 'You look fucking amazing tonight.' Nico was mesmerised by the sight of this beauty in front of him.

Scarlotte watched her friend flirt outrageously with

Nico. Ali was the queen of flirting and Scarlotte knew she could learn a thing or two from her best friend. Nico had his hand on Ali's knee, and she would slap his thigh each time he made a cheeky comment to her. Their stools got closer together, and their body language showed that they were both interested in each other as Ali's knees rested on the inside of Nico's.

'Meet me after work tonight. I will take you for a drink,' Nico said to Ali as she prepared to leave.

'OK, I'll come back here when I've finished,' she replied as Nico pulled her towards him and planted a big kiss on her cheek and then nuzzled his nose into her neck. Ali wrapped one leg around his body, and she returned the cuddle with enthusiasm. Scarlotte could tell that she was most definitely up for a night of passion with Nico.

'See you later!' Ali shouted to Scarlotte as she left Cafe Marina with a spring in her step.

'Bye, Ali.' Scarlotte was collecting glasses from outside the bar and gave her friend a big meaningful grin.

'I think I'm in love,' Nico said to Scarlotte as she put the empty glasses in the sink to be washed. 'Does she really like me? I can't tell if she is just messing around, you know.' Nico felt a little insecure when it came to Ali. He really liked her a lot but also feared that the feeling wasn't genuinely mutual.

'Well, she's meeting you tonight, so that's a good sign, eh?' Scarlotte replied as she pushed the top of a glass into the cleaning bristles of the pot washer.

Nico was in the best mood tonight; he laughed and joked with the customers. Scarlotte could see how excited he was to finally be having a real date with Ali. She herself was planning to have an early night tonight so she would be all fresh for the workers' party tomorrow. She felt weary and was looking forward to having the apartment to herself for the evening and getting a good night's sleep.

'Hello, gorgeous.' Scarlotte had her head down washing

glasses behind the bar. She looked up to see the blond guy from the shop opposite Manoli sitting at the bar in front of her. Her heart skipped a beat; he was looking really handsome tonight. His blond hair was all clean and fluffy, he wore a white fitted T-shirt which showed off his muscular torso, and dark blue jeans. He was smiling widely at Scarlotte as he ordered an Ouzo from Leo.

'Oh, er, hi. How are you?' Scarlotte tripped over her words as she replied. She didn't know why but she found this guy mysterious and he seemed somehow different from other guys she had met on the island. He held out his hand to Scarlotte.

'I am Dimitri, pleased to meet you properly, Scarlotte.' He already knew her name which didn't surprise her.

Scarlotte wiped her wet hands on her jeans and shook Dimitri's hand. He held onto her hand a little longer than a normal greeting handshake and gazed into her eyes, making her blush from the neck upwards. Putting her head down again to try to hide her blushes, Scarlotte continued with her work. Nico pulled up a stool next to Dimitri and they sat chatting for a while. Scarlotte could tell that they were talking about her by the way they would look around at her as Nico slapped Dimitri on the shoulder.

'Hey, darlin', Dimitri wants to take you out after work.' Nico couldn't help himself from being the matchmaker, especially as he knew that Ali would be otherwise engaged this evening.

Scarlotte stood next to Nico as Dimitri looked at her, waiting for a reply. 'Um OK, yeah, sure,' she replied as Nico scuttled off leaving her alone with Dimitri.

Dimitri downed the last of his Ouzo and stood up to leave. 'I'll come back here when I close my shop and I'll take you over to Kos Town.' Kissing Scarlotte on the cheek, he swiftly left the bar before she could change her mind.

'Bloody hell, Nico, I didn't get much chance to think about that, did I?' she said to Nico as he came back to the bar.

The big guy put his arm around her shoulder. 'He's all right, Scarlotte. He will look after you, I promise.' He then winked at her.

'There'll be none of that funny business, I can assure you,' she said stiffly.

'OK, darling, but I can't say the same for me and Ali tonight,' he teased as he jokingly punched her on the arm before going outside to entertain his customers.

Scarlotte had mixed feelings about going out with Dimitri that evening. She found him attractive and a little quirky-looking, which interested her, but she had also been looking forward to an early night alone. Oh well, she would go with the flow as she always did and try to enjoy the evening whatever it flung at her.

*

Dimitri arrived back at Cafe Marina around midnight just as the music was being turned off.

He had obviously been home and changed after closing his shop, as he wore a fresh dark blue T-shirt and lighter blue jeans, and had trendy white trainers on his feet with no socks - yes, NO SOCKS! Scarlotte didn't understand how men could do this. Surely they would get smelly, sweaty feet? She wondered if Dimitri's feet smelt and gagged at the thought.

Dimitri gave Scarlotte another kiss on her cheek and sat down on the same stool as earlier.

'You can go now, Scarlotte. It's not too busy and Leo and I can manage.' Nico seemed very keen to let Dimitri take her off for a night out, she thought.

'OK, thanks.' Scarlotte scuttled off to the toilet to have a wee and check herself in the mirror. She didn't look too bad considering she'd just finished work, and thankfully she had worn her favourite leopard-print vest top which looked good with her skinny jeans. She brushed her hair and sniffed her armpits to make sure that she didn't smell of body odour, washed her hands and took a deep breath before joining Dimitri at the bar.

'OK, let's go.' Dimitri stood up and offered Scarlotte his hand.

'Look after Ali tonight and tell her where I've gone, please!' Scarlotte shouted to Nico as she left hand-in-hand with Dimitri.

Dimitri's car was just around the corner in one of the back streets. It was a dusty silver saloon and had seen better days. I bet this heap of junk wouldn't pass an MOT back at home, Scarlotte thought as Dimitri opened the passenger door for her. However, the car was spotless inside and the seats were comfy. An air freshener hung from the mirror. 'Mmm, that smells lovely,' she said as Dimitri climbed in next to her.

'Thank you, darling, so do you.' She knew he didn't mean that because she'd been working all night and probably reeked of fags, stale beer and cleaning fluid.

As Dimitri pulled away, Scarlotte faced the window, cupped her left hand over her mouth and breathed in it to see if she had fag breath. It wasn't too bad, but she could do with a mint. She fumbled around in her bumbag (which she had forgotten to take off after work), looking for a mint. God, what the hell do I look like with this stupid bag on? she thought as she found a packet of chewing gum in the small zip pocket at the front.

'Want one?' She held the screwed-up packet over to Dimitri who just looked at it with disgust and politely declined.

Scarlotte felt surprisingly comfortable in Dimitri's company as they chatted about his shop, his family and life on Kos. Dimitri had been born in Athens; his dad was Greek, and his mum was German, which explained the blond hair. His parents had met when his mum had been back-packing around Greece when she was younger, and just after a year they had been married. He now lived with them in Kos in a villa on the edge of their resort. The shop was owned by them, but Dimitri ran it. His English was particularly good, much better than Manoli's.

The journey to Kos Town would only take twenty minutes and Scarlotte thought that the car would just about manage this short journey as it rattled along the bumpy, dusty roads.

'So, why did you go out with Manoli?' Dimitri asked Scarlotte as they pulled up outside a little Greek bar in Kos Town. 'I think he's not really your type.'

'Why do you think that?' She had never heard anyone say that before.

'Well, he never goes out, he doesn't really drink and all he does is work. He *really* doesn't seem like your type, Scarlotte.' Well, that was all true to be honest, but she wouldn't say she really had a *type*.

'He's a lovely man, Dimitri, just not right for me at this moment in time. I like to go out and have fun and you're right, he is dedicated to his work,' Scarlotte replied as Dimitri pulled back a chair outside the bar for her to sit on.

Dimitri ordered them both an Ouzo with water and sat down opposite her. His eyes were piecing blue and she hadn't realised just how wide his face was before - almost on a par with a full moon but without the craters. His skin was a light golden-brown and looked really healthy. I bet he moisturises, she thought, and pictured his bathroom cabinet being full of expensive male-grooming products.

The conversation flowed between them as they sat people-watching outside the bar. Each time Dimitri got up to go to the bar or the bathroom, he would shift his chair closer to Scarlotte's. Sit on my knee, why don't you, went through her mind as his chair arm nudged hers. She did actually like it if she was honest, and he was close enough now for her to smell his aftershave and the Ouzo on his breath.

'Come back to mine, Scarlotte. I will show you our

villa,' he whispered in her ear in his deep breathy voice.

That's a new one, she thought. Usually guys would ask you to come back for a coffee, wouldn't they? She knew exactly where this was going, and after all, she did fancy him - so why not.

They arrived at the villa half an hour later. It was two o'clock in the morning and Scarlotte yawned all the way there.

'Are you tired, darling? Maybe you should have a lie-down.'

This guy knows all the tricks of the trade, she thought as she climbed out of the dusty saloon.

The villa was detached with gardens surrounding the outside. The building was white in the traditional Greek style with a wooden blue door. Dimitri held his forefinger up to his lips to signal that they must be quiet as his parents would no doubt be sleeping. The hallway inside the front door was small and very tidy. The walls were white, and the floor covering was a highly polished cream tiling. There were no shoes strewn about the floor as there were in her and Ali's apartment. The stairway was to the right of the hallway and they tiptoed up to Dimitri's room which was the second room on the left.

His room consisted of a medium-sized bed with a plain blue quilt, a white chest of drawers and matching wardrobe. It was extremely basic, no pictures hanging on the wall or any type of decor. It was just plain, tidy and masculine.

'Wow, it's so hot,' Scarlotte said, wiping her brow as she stood waiting for his first move. She could feel the sexual tension between them and knew that they would soon be ruffling that neatly ironed quilt cover.

'Maybe you should take this off.' Dimitri kissed Scarlotte passionately on the lips before lifting her top over her head. She returned the kiss with equal enthusiasm and let him strip her of her clothes. Scarlotte then fumbled with his belt but couldn't get it undone, so Dimitri assisted then quickly whipped off the rest of his clothes.

They spent the next couple of hours making love until Dimitri had run out of condoms. It was great sex and he definitely knew what he was doing.

'I'd better take you home, darling, before my parents wake up.' He was nuzzled behind Scarlotte, breathing in the scent of her long blonde hair. He removed his arm from around her waist and stroked his fingers down her naked back.

They crept out of the bedroom and down the stairs, back outside to the car. They were both now really knackered, and it was a good job the car ride back was only five minutes.

'Thank you for an amazing night.' Dimitri leaned over and kissed Scarlotte on the cheek.

'See you soon,' she replied as she climbed out of the car and tiredly walked up the stairs to her apartment.

Chapter Twenty-nine

Scarlotte woke later that morning to find that Ali was still not back from her date with Nico.

For a brief moment, last night's shenanigans had slipped her mind as she rolled over to get comfy for another hour's kip.

'MORNING.' Ali burst into the room, full of beans as usual.

'Ugh, God, what time is it?' Scarlotte rolled back over to see her friend looking rather bedraggled. Ali's T-shirt was on inside out and her hair was all messy.

'Never mind what time it is. Haven't you got some gossip for me?' Ali jumped on Scarlotte's bed, eager to hear last night's news.

'Ouch, watch my bloody legs! You don't want to be pushing me around in a wheelchair, do you?' Scarlotte wriggled herself into a sitting position, releasing her legs from the weight of Ali's bum. 'Anyway, why don't you start. Look at your bloody T-shirt! You put that on in a hurry this morning, didn't you?' She tweaked on the tag sticking out of the side of Ali's T-shirt.

'Oh my God, Scarlotte, he didn't let me sleep all night. We only went for one drink and then back to his place.' This sounded remarkably familiar to Scarlotte.

'Sooo - do you like him? I mean *really* like him, Ali?'

'He's funny, but I don't know if I really fancy him.' Ali went into detail about her passionate night with Nico and how he had a 'large willy' as she called it. Then she asked: 'So, come on then. Nico told me that you went out with that blond guy. Did he get rid of those cobwebs in your knickers?' She listened intently with mouth wide open at some points, as Scarlotte filled her in on her evening with Dimitri.

'And you were going to have an early night, you dirty stop-out.' Ali yawned and lay back on Scarlotte's bed. They'd both had a good night but now they desperately needed to get a couple of hours' kip before the workers' party later that day.

*

There was a big crowd of workers already outside Poppers when they arrived at around 2 p.m. Many of them were already drunk and the girls had heard the noise well before they reached the front strip. As they walked into sight, there was a burst of applause from inside Poppers which made everyone else look at them. The watersports guys were all sitting together drinking bottles of beer and generally being loud and raucous. Scarlotte felt embarrassed as she didn't like to be the centre of attention in such a large crowd.

It didn't take long for Ali and Scarlotte to be surrounded by guys who also worked on the island. Some of them they had not seen before, and some had familiar faces. They chatted to four guys who worked on the watersports at the next town who had joined the party and Scarlotte was invited by one of them to spend the day on the beach with him. Spencer, who was tall, bronzed, toned and bloody gorgeous with his shoulder-length bleached surfer's hair, had made a beeline for Scarlotte. He was wearing funky, brightly coloured boardshorts and flipflops. His chest was bare and Scarlotte thought that he wouldn't look out of place on the cover of a men's fitness magazine. His mates had wandered off to chat to other workers and Ali had disappeared off somewhere to no doubt utilise her amazing flirting skills.

'Come over to the beach tomorrow. It'll be fun, I promise. I can collect you in the speedboat from the watersports beach here.' Spencer had a very deep, manly British voice which really was irresistible. His gaze into Scarlotte's eyes did not waver even when a group of fit babes walked past them in bikinis.

'Oi oi, Scarlotte!' Slapping her back, Drake had joined the party with the other two boys close behind him.

'Hi, mate.' Drake shook Spencer's hand.

'I'll pick you up at eleven then,' Spencer said as he left Scarlotte to chat with her buddies.

'OK, great. I'll be there.' Scarlotte pointed to the beach hut where the watersports were situated.

'Ooh, have you got a date?' Drake teased, putting his arm around her shoulder. He and Darren had been drinking since noon and were already the worse for wear.

'We've arranged to get the night off tonight,' he went on, 'so why don't you and Ali do the same? Greg is off too, and we can all go out together.' Drake looked at Scarlotte expectantly. She thought this did sound like a great idea.

The three of them went on the hunt for Ali and found her chatting to some guys who were on holiday and gatecrashing the workers' party. After being peeled away from the group, Ali also thought this was a great idea, so she and Scarlotte nipped off to get permission from their respective bosses. Ali got permission straight away, but Nico was not so easy to persuade. Scarlotte felt bad for asking him but she was desperate to go out for just one night with her friends. As Ali was with her, she used her friend's flirting skills to assist, and it wasn't long before Nico succumbed to her charms and agreed to let Scarlotte play out with her friends that night.

Both were feeling extremely excited at the prospect of going out that night and quickly headed back to the party to break the good news to the others. As they arrived, a local photographer was getting the crowd together for a workers' photo. Everyone was squashing up together outside Poppers to ensure that they appeared in this year's photo. Ali and Scarlotte squeezed themselves in at the right of the group. They would have liked to be next to the boys, but they couldn't see them. The photo would be put up in a shop just off the square and could be purchased for a couple of drachmas. Scarlotte would definitely buy a copy to add to her little box of memories.

After the crowd dispersed, they found Darren and Drake, who had apparently pushed to the front of the crowd for the photo and were sitting on the ground. No wonder they couldn't find them. So, after the excitement of the group photo, it was agreed that they would all meet at 7 p.m. at Adelphia and eat before they hit the bars.

Chapter Thirty

Ali and Scarlotte hadn't had too much to drink in the day because they wanted to be feeling fresh for their first proper full night out with all of the gang. They were back in their apartment for 5 p.m. which would give them enough time to shower, do their hair, choose outfits (which would of course take up most of the time) and apply their make-up.

'Who was that surfer dude you were talking to this afternoon? He's bloody gorgeous!' Ali shouted from her room as she put on her lipstick in the mirror.

'He works at the watersports on the next beach along from ours. He's picking me up tomorrow and - wait for it – he's coming in a speedboat.' Scarlotte was feeling really cool about being picked up in a boat. No clapped-out saloon car in sight this time.

'Oooh, that sounds really exciting.' Ali got up from the dressing-table and started to search through her wardrobe for something to wear. 'What about Dimitri? Will you be seeing him again?'

Scarlotte hadn't made any plans to meet up with Dimitri again. She wasn't that bothered though as the prospect of spending the day at the watersports with Spencer was far more appealing.

They left the apartment just before 7 p.m. and headed to Adelphia to meet the boys. Greg was sitting at one of the tables having a beer and enjoying a bit of peace and quiet on his own.

'Evening, Greg,' Ali said in her strong Brummie voice as she sat down next to him. Scarlotte sat opposite Greg and gave him a wink. 'Where's Drake and Darren?' she asked after ordering a beer for herself and Ali from the waiter.

Drake and Darren hadn't got back from the workers'

party until 6.30 p.m., Greg said, so they were still getting ready. Drake was also bringing along another friend called Caroline who was working in the same Chinese restaurant as him.

'They'll be here in half an hour,' Greg told them, looking at his fake gold Rolex watch to check the time.

They sat chatting for an hour before the boys turned up with Caroline. Ali and Scarlotte hadn't met her before but they had seen her around the resort.

'Hi, everyone,' Darren said as the three of them joined the table.

Drake introduced Caroline to Ali and Scarlotte. She was from London and working in Greece for her gap year. She also had blonde hair which reached her shoulders and was styled straight with a centre parting. She was quite petite at only about 5 feet 4 inches in height. Her eyes were brown and her smile was wide, revealing lovely straight white teeth. Ali and Scarlotte instantly warmed to her.

They ordered their food whilst chatting and laughing about what they had been up to that day at the party. The boys discussed which girls at the party were fit, and which were not as fit, or as they called it 'shaggable or not shaggable'. None of them had 'scored' at the party, however, because there was far too much competition.

'You'll just have me for company on the beach tomorrow, because this one' – here Ali pointed to Scarlotte – 'is being picked up in a speedboat for a date.'

'Ooh, you kept that quiet. Who is picking you up?' Greg asked. He felt a bit jealous because he secretly had a soft spot for Scarlotte.

Knowing that Greg liked her and not wishing to make him feel bad, she played it down and replied that she was just hanging out with the guys who worked on the watersports in the next resort - it was no big deal. Inside, though, Scarlotte felt really excited at the prospect of spending the day with the gorgeous beach-bum Spencer.

After finishing their meal together, the six of them found the nearest bar to start what would turn out to be one of the best evenings they had had all season. They found a bar with enough seats outside to accommodate the six of them. Being workers in the resort, they would never pay full price for drinks which meant that they could all get sozzled without either breaking the bank or using any of the money they had saved for their flights home at the end of the season. They all stuck to beer for now because mixing their drinks too early would no doubt end up with one of them being sick or being carried home by the rest of the gang.

'Want me to hypnotise you, Ali?' Greg asked as he took a swig from his beer bottle.

'Hypnotise her?' Scarlotte repeated. 'You're not going to put her in a trance and make her walk around like a chicken, are you?' She had seen this done before on the telly and was never sure whether the person being hypnotised was just acting or actually under hypnosis.

'No, I won't make her do that, I promise.' Greg pulled his seat opposite Ali's and asked Scarlotte if he could borrow her lighter. The rest of them gathered around, eager not to miss this spectacle.

Greg sat knee-to-knee with Ali and asked her if she was ready. 'I need you to relax now,' he said as he held the bottle of beer in front of Ali's face and lit the flame of the lighter underneath the glass bottle.

'Keep looking at the top of the bottle, Ali, don't take your eyes off it. Try to relax and stop laughing, please - this is serious stuff.' Ali couldn't help but giggle as Greg started to put on a calming hypnotist voice which sounded even more funny in his Scouser accent.

'Now close your eyes, Ali, as I take you into trance.' Scarlotte burst out laughing, at which Greg put his forefinger to his lips to ask her to be quiet.

Ali closed her eyes and Greg signalled to the group to remain silent. With the flame now extinguished, he rubbed his fingers on the bottom of the bottle and then slowly ran his fingers down Ali's cheeks and across her forehead.

'Remain still . . . you are starting to feel really sleepy . . . just relax and feel my fingers calming you into a deep trance.' Greg was really enjoying his show but Ali wasn't taking it seriously and kept giggling.

The group could now see why Greg had used the beer bottle and the flame of the lighter because his 'relaxing fingers' were actually covered in soot from the bottom of the bottle. Ali's face was now also covered in stripes of the black soot!

She is going to bloody kill you, Scarlotte thought as she looked at the rest of the gang. Darren had had to walk off because he could not contain his laughter any longer. Scarlotte could not make eye contact with Drake because she knew that the laugh held in her throat would burst out.

'How do you feel, Ali? Do you feel all relaxed now?' Greg maintained his professional hypnotist stance as Ali opened her eyes.

'Well, that was a bloody waste of time, Greg. I don't feel any different. Pass me my beer.' Ali reached over to the table and grabbed her beer, little knowing that she had been transformed into a coal miner who had just finished a long shift down the pit.

'Don't let her go to the toilet,' Greg murmured in Scarlotte's ear.

'You know she's going to murder you, Greg, don't you?' Scarlotte felt bad for her friend but it was hilarious, and she knew Ali would take it in good spirits.

They left the bar with coal miner Ali, who was none the wiser about the black soot on her face, apart from feeling a bit paranoid that people kept looking at her.

They walked through the town to the next bar and ordered shots this time to accompany their beer.

'Just going for a wee,' Ali announced as she stood up from their outside seats and was off before Scarlotte was able to stop her. Greg looked at Scarlotte with horror – well, not really with horror, more amusement that Ali was going to see her face in the mirror. They all sat quietly, waiting for the explosion – and it was only a moment before a screech came from the toilets.

'You bastard, Greg!' Ali ran out of the toilets, her hands covering her face. 'Oh my God - look at me! No wonder people were staring at me.' She smacked Greg on the arm, leaving sooty fingerprints on his top. They were all crying with laughter, including Ali who now had more stripes down her sooty face from the tears of laughter.

'I'm going to wash it off.' She stuck two fingers up at Greg as she stomped her way back to the toilets. It was almost as funny as the time they sank the pedalo, Scarlotte thought, as she followed her friend to the cloakroom to help her remove the black from her face.

The night was still young, and they already were having the best time together. Ali had cleaned her face and applied some fresh lipstick, so she looked her usual self again. Four bars and many shots later it was time to head off to a club. They decided that Star would be the choice of venue for tonight. Ali, Scarlotte and Caroline danced the night away as the boys flitted around the place chatting to numerous girls. Some of the other workers had made their way up to the club too and there was a real sense of community when they were all together.

At 3 a.m. they left the club and needed to find a place where they could eat to soak up the alcohol they had imbibed that evening.

'Let's go to the Soup Kitchen,' Drake slurred as he linked arms with Caroline. The place was near to Star, and just down the road from Scarlotte and Ali's apartment. It was always open until around 4 a.m., so they should be able to get a feed before they closed. It was really busy when they arrived, but they managed to find a table for four and squeezed a couple of extra chairs around it. Being a soup kitchen there wasn't a wide variety of culinary delights to choose from. There was soup or soup - or soup.

'I think I'll have soup,' Greg announced after looking at the menu, which made them all laugh.

Scarlotte had ordered chicken soup which was basically flavoured water with a few bits of chicken floating around in it. It was tasty though and the chicken was soft and tender, well, the two pieces she found were anyway. Ali had tomato soup, which was equally watery, definitely not creamy Heinz Tomato Soup.

Greg yawned after finishing his soup, which made everyone else yawn.

'Time for bed, I think,' Darren said as he stood up to leave. The rest of them followed him out to see the golden sun just poking its nose up from the horizon. It had been a great night and everyone had massive smiles on their faces as they cuddled and said their goodnights.

Chapter Thirty-one

Scarlotte woke feeling like a bear with a sore head from last night's shenanigans. Initially when she woke it had slipped her mind that she would be needing to get herself down to the beach to meet Spencer that morning. She sat up in bed and rubbed her tired eyes, trying desperately to focus, and once firmly on two feet she popped her head around Ali's bedroom door to check on her. Ali was fast asleep; she was still fully clothed and had one shoe on, which made Scarlotte snigger.

Making a coffee and going out to the balcony was so much easier now that they had separate bedrooms. Early riser Scarlotte didn't need to sneak around like Inspector Clouseau on a secret mission to avoid waking the suspect - which in this particular case was Ali.

It was another scorching hot day and the prospect of spending all day with the gorgeous Spencer was definitely appealing.

She had a good hour or so before she would need to leave, which was plenty of time to down a couple of paracetamols, eat something sugary and rehydrate with a gallon of coffee.

Ali woke up just as Scarlotte was about to leave. She hobbled out of her room with the one shoe still on her right foot.

'Oooh, you look gorgeous,' she said, adding, 'lip gloss in the daytime too - hey!' Scarlotte was wearing her white bikini with a white T-shirt tied around her waist and her wedged sandals to make her even taller. She had washed her hair and applied just a little lip gloss which would hopefully entice Spencer to kiss her.

'Just making an effort ready to be picked up in the speedboat. I like your sleepwear, by the way.' Scarlotte pointed to Ali's feet which made them both laugh.

Leaning against the doorframe to remove the one shoe, and then almost falling over, Ali said she was going back to bed for an hour as she still felt rough from last night. She then tripped over the discarded shoe and banged her little toe on the bedframe which made her swear.

'Bloody hell, Ali,' Scarlotte said, 'I think you'd be safer on the beach, you piss-head.'

Ali grumbled something as she pulled the bedsheet over her head.

'See you later, mate,' Scarlotte shouted as she left to meet Spencer. There was no answer from her friend as she had fallen into a comatose sleep, half on and half off her bed.

*

Scarlotte could hear the speedboat bouncing along the waves towards their meeting point. Spencer was exactly on time to collect her. He looked so bloody gorgeous steering the speedboat bare-chested with his shoulder-length surfer hair blowing in the wind. Scarlotte imagined the whole episode in slow motion with the latest James Bond theme music playing in the background as he brought the boat to a stop on the beach edge. She felt like a movie star as jealous onlookers watched her hunk of a guy help her to climb onboard. She was definitely living her best life!

'Hey, darling. I am so pleased you're here. We need to dash back to the watersports because I have to take some customers out paragliding, and then I'll be free. You can hang out with the gang until I get back in.'

'Yeah, sure,' Scarlotte replied as she took the seat next to Captain Gorgeous.

The noise of the engine made it difficult to talk, so Scarlotte just kept glancing over at the beautiful body of Spencer as he bounced the boat over the waves to the next resort. His arms were strong, and his torso was ripped to the max. She wondered if it would be appropriate to stroke his body at this moment in time but decided that it might be a bit too forward at this early stage in their relationship. Not that they were in a relationship in the real world, just in her head.

When they arrived at the next beach resort, Spencer introduced Scarlotte to 'the gang' who were all surfer dudes. They were perched on chairs in the shade under a wooden hut with a straw roof. She felt a little bit self-conscious being the only female there, but the boys soon made her feel comfortable and chatted about themselves and where they were from. One of the guys was called Jason and he thoughtfully handed her a cold can of lemon pop. He was particularly cool, Scarlotte thought. He travelled throughout the whole year spending the summers in Europe and then the winter surfing in Australia, which was his home country. What a life! Scarlotte wondered what she would be doing at the end of this season back in England with the rain, snow, hail and God knows what else the weather would bring. She momentarily shivered at the thought.

Spencer was only out for an hour with the paragliding holidaymakers. They arrived back on the beach looking a little queasy from being buffeted around by the wind whilst attached to a massive parachute.

'They always look green around the gills after paragliding on a windy day,' Jason said to Scarlotte out of earshot of the customers, as she watched Spencer help them out of their harnesses.

'Not sure I'd fancy it in this wind either, especially after a night out on the razz.' She took a sip of her lemon pop to try to take away the taste of the chicken soup from last night which was repeating on her.

Once the happy, yet slightly green holidaymakers had been given their photos of their kamikaze ride, Spencer was now free to join them. He pulled up a chair next to Scarlotte and opened a can for himself. They chatted comfortably to each other, like old friends really. He was so easy to talk to, and what she liked about him was that he wasn't trying to come on to her or making crude innuendos - which was as refreshing as the lemon pop.

'Hey Spencer, when are we going to do it?' The wind had dropped a bit now and Jason seemed eager to do whatever *it* was that they had planned.

'Seems like a good time now, dude, don't you think?' Spencer gave Scarlotte a wink as he and Jason got up from their seats.

'What on earth are you two up to?' she asked, mock-frowning at them play-fighting with each other.

'You'll see,' Spencer replied as he and Jason got up and ran towards the speedboat, trying to trip each other up on the way. They climbed aboard the boat and Spencer took them out about 200 metres from the shore.

'Wait until you see what these two nutcases get up to,' one of the other guys said to Scarlotte.

'They're proper thrill-seekers and absolutely bonkers,' another added.

Scarlotte could see them preparing the large blue and white striped parachute and it looked like Spencer was helping Jason into a harness. Spencer started to release the parachute with Jason attached to the bottom of it. The line seemed to go up and up and up, high in the sky. She could hear Jason and Spencer shouting to each other but couldn't quite make out what they were saying, apart from Spencer bellowing, 'High enough, dude?'

At this point, Scarlotte hadn't noticed that Jason was not in fact strapped into a harness; he was just holding onto the ropes under the parachute with his bare hands. This only became totally apparent when Jason let go of the ropes and plunged from what seemed like miles up in the sky into the deep sea.

'Wooo-hooo!' he screamed as he fell and made a big splash into the sea.

'Oh my God!' Scarlotte stood up and joined in with a round of applause from the gang. Jason popped up from under the sea and gave the thumbs-up to signal that he was OK – well, to signal that he was actually still alive would be more accurate.

Spencer reeled in the parachute and spun the boat around to pick up Jason who was bobbing around in the water.

'I think that's the highest yet.' Jason looked incredibly pleased with himself as they both jogged back up the beach.

'You mean you've done that before?' Scarlotte asked, looking a little shell-shocked.

'Yeah, most days when we get the chance. Do you want to have a go?'

'Erm, let me think about that for a second . . . NO BLOODY WAY, you nutters.'

They all chatted together for the next couple of hours until Scarlotte asked if Spencer would drop her off as she needed to get ready for work. The trip back to her resort was just as pleasurable as the journey that morning.

'I'll come over to see you in your bar later,' Spencer said as he kissed her cheek before lending her a hand off the speedboat.

'OK, great. I'll see you later then.' Scarlotte stood on the beach and waved to Spencer as he spun the boat around and sped off into the sea.

Chapter Thirty-two

Ali was in the apartment when Scarlotte arrived back from her beach trip with Spencer.

'Hiya!' she shouted as she locked the front door behind her.

'I'm in here.' Ali was in her own room, flat out on the bed.

'Have you actually got up today?' Scarlotte asked as she sat on the bottom of Ali's bed.

'No, I felt too rough from last night. Anyway, more importantly, how was your day? Tell me all of the gossip.' Ali listened with interest as Scarlotte told her how Spencer had picked her up in the boat and about the parachute drop into the sea. 'Wow, they sound mental,' she said. 'Will you see him again?'

'He said he's coming over to the bar tonight.' Scarlotte had a big silly grin on her face.

'Well, I said I'd meet Nico tonight after work, so I guess I'll not be getting much sleep again.' Ali did a massive yawn and closed her eyes.

'Come on, get in the shower and I'll make you a coffee.' Scarlotte went off to put the kettle on and make them both a much-needed cup of sugary (in Ali's case) caffeine.

*

Scarlotte was delighted to find that Nico's mum had sent over a plate of food for them all to eat whilst at work that evening. There were pork skewers with onions, homemade stuffed vine leaves and delicious warm bread. Nico's mum was the best cook and her dolmades were to die for. Scarlotte would stuff at least ten of them in her face before she started work.

Nico was in a joyous mood again because of his pending date with Ali that evening. He was full of life and the customers loved him.

Tonight, Scarlotte was wearing her dark blue jeans, the shoes that Manoli had bought her and a red bra top with tassels hanging all the way around and which reached her belly button. She had taken a little extra time in the mirror tonight to ensure that she looked her best for Spencer.

The bar was so busy, and the time just flew away with itself. It was midnight before they knew it and the music was turned down. The police had been walking around the bars tonight to ensure that music was turned off; they also checked that receipts were being given to customers and that workers had a Green Card, allowing them to actually be working. Neither Scarlotte nor Ali had a Green Card, nor to be fair did any of the other workers that they knew. Whenever word got round from other bar-owners that the police were about, the workers would just mingle in with the customers, pretending to be holidaymakers. There was never a problem though and the police would just pop in and out of each bar. No one ever got into trouble and the police were more bothered about the music curfew than anything else.

Scarlotte had given up hope of Spencer coming to see her until he appeared at half-past midnight, saying, 'Sorry I'm so late, darling. The truth is, I fell asleep.' He gave Scarlotte a kiss on the cheek and sat himself down on a stool by the bar. He looked bloody gorgeous in his shorts and Hawaiian shirt; of course, he was still wearing his flipflops which were a compulsory item of clothing for a surfer dude. They chatted whilst he played with the tassels on her top, flicking them with his fingers and occasionally letting them touch her slim waist, which made her skin tingle.

'Come over to my place after work,' Spencer whispered in Scarlotte's ear as he put his arm around her waist and pulled her towards him. He gave her instructions of where his apartment was; surprisingly, it was only two streets away from Cafe Marina. He would wait up for her, he said, and would have a glass of something delicious waiting for them to drink together on the balcony. He finished his drink and, seeing that Scarlotte was still busy, he kissed her goodbye and went home.

After being teased about Spencer for the next hour by Nico, the bar was ready to be closed. The final customers left at around 1.30 a.m., allowing them to start to clean up.

Ali arrived just as they were putting away the chairs and kindly gave them a hand to speed up the process. Nico was planning to take Ali out for a drink in one of the busier bars which would still be open, and Scarlotte would go on a hunt for Spencer's place.

'Want me to come with you?' Ali asked as they stood outside waiting for Nico to lock up.

'No, I'll be fine. He only lives a couple of streets away. I'm sure I'll find it.'

There were no street names or house numbers, so Scarlotte had to go purely on the description of the street and the door. She was looking for a street where the end house had blue pots with flowers on the windowsill (not uncommon in Greece, she thought) and his door was the second one along on the left and was painted yellow. It led to a staircase, and his room would be the second door along. Scarlotte walked up and down streets and couldn't find a yellow door anywhere. She was also a bit worried about ending up in the wrong apartment and frightening the life out of some unsuspecting Greek family who would be tucked up in bed.

After half an hour of wandering around, Scarlotte gave up. She was knackered anyway and could do with going to bed. She would just have to explain to Spencer that she couldn't find his place and ask him to draw her a map for next time.

Feeling a little bit frustrated and worried that Spencer would think that she wasn't interested, she plodded tiredly back up the hill to the apartment. She knew that Ali would still be out with Nico so she decided she would just have a last cigarette on the balcony in the warm night air and then get a good night's sleep. She was looking forward to having a normal day on the beach in the morning with the gang and as it was Ali's birthday, they would be able to celebrate all together. Scarlotte had got Ali's card on the way back from the beach yesterday. They had agreed not to buy presents because they didn't really have the money, but Scarlotte would make sure that her friend had fun on her special day.

As she climbed wearily into bed, the apartment was lovely and quiet and all she could hear was the chirping of crickets, a sound which would always send her off into a deep sleep.

Chapter Thirty-three

'HAPPY BIRTHDAY!' Scarlotte burst into Ali's room and leapt onto her bed. 'Open your card, you dirty stop-out. What time did you get in?'

Ali slowly emerged from under her white crumpled sheet with her make-up still on from last night. Her hair was all over the place and her mascara was so smudged that she looked like Alice Cooper's side-kick.

'Ah, thank you. And a good morning to you too.' Ali leant up on one elbow, yawned and opened her card. 'I don't know what time it was when I got in, it was light though.' She gave Scarlotte a big hug and placed the card on her bedside table.

'What would you like to do today, Birthday Girl? Do you want to go down to the beach and spend the day with the boys?'

'Yes, please. We've not had a proper beach day with them for a few days, so I reckon that would be simply perfect.' Ali managed to sit herself up then spotted her reflection in the mirror. 'Bloody hell, what do I look like,' she laughed as she tried to wipe the mascara from under her eyes.

'You look gorgeous, as usual. Right, while you wake up properly I'm going to make you a birthday breakfast.' Scarlotte got up and went to the kitchen to see what she could find. She laid out the table on the balcony and put two large glasses of orange juice for them to enjoy with their food There was some bread in the freezer which was still in date - most unusual for them as they rarely ate in the apartment, some eggs - and yay! - a packet of bacon.

Scarlotte busied herself in the kitchen whilst Ali pulled herself out of her bed and washed the make-up off her face.

'Birthday breakfast is ready!' Scarlotte shouted from the

kitchen as she placed their two plates on the balcony table.

'Ooh, it smells delicious.' Ali plonked herself down opposite Scarlotte and attacked her bacon and eggs on toast.

'We should do this more often. It would save us some money,' Scarlotte said as she stuffed the last bit of cremated bacon in her mouth.

'Could do with some red sauce though,' Ali said.

'RED sauce? On bacon? No, no, *no*, Ali. Brown sauce goes on bacon, you monster.'

'WHAT! Don't be ridiculous, girl,' Ali argued, a big grin on her face. 'Everyone knows that red sauce goes on bacon!'

They spent the next five minutes having the brown sauce v. red sauce debate and finally agreed they would ask the boys their opinion later, which would settle the argument.

After washing up together they got themselves ready, fetched their Lilos and headed for the beach.

During the walk, Scarlotte told Ali about her unsuccessful treasure hunt last night and her fear that the pot of gold called Spencer would think she wasn't interested. She wondered whether he would come over to the bar that night to find out why she hadn't turned up.

'Aw, that's a shame,' Ali sympathised. 'He is really hot, isn't he? I reckon he totally likes you so I wouldn't worry about it. If he doesn't come and see you later, we'll just have to go over to their resort tomorrow and seek him out.' She gave Scarlotte a consoling hug around her waist, which meant she dropped her Lilo on the ground. Fortunately, they both managed to grab it at the same time before it flew off and battered another unsuspecting elderly Greek man on the bonce.

The boys hadn't arrived at the beach by the time they got there, so they had first dibs on the sunbeds. Stuffing their Lilos underneath, the girls settled down for a snooze in the morning sunshine. Scarlotte looked up at the clear blue sky and felt a real sense of contentment. Life could not be any better and she never wanted this time to end.

Both girls drifted off into a lovely deep sleep which they definitely needed after having some very late nights recently. Time passed, and it wasn't until midday that they were woken up by the sound of the boys singing 'Happy Birthday' out of tune as they approached the beach.

'Wahey! Happy Birthday!' Greg leapt onto Ali's sunbed and gave her a cuddle.

Darren and Drake put down a white carrier bag next to Scarlotte's bed and went around to wish Ali a Happy Birthday.

'Ah, thanks, you lot,' Ali said as she rearranged her bikini top which had exposed her left boob after the cuddles.

'Calm down, Ali,' Darren piped up. 'Keep your clothes on, I've only just got here.' She slapped him on the arm playfully.

'How do you girls fancy a barbecue?' Greg asked. 'We've been shopping to get food and a disposable barbecue for the Birthday Girl. We'll just need to move to the quiet beach further down there.' He pointed in the direction of the quiet beach which was a two-minute walk.

'Sounds AMAZING!' Ali sat up and clapped her hands together, giving Scarlotte a big smile.

Drake had been shopping that morning and had purchased burgers, chicken skewers, salad and bread rolls. As he worked in a restaurant, he was the nearest thing to the chef in the group, even though he was only a pot-washer.

They moved their stuff over to the next beach which was quiet as they had expected. There were no sunbeds here, and only the odd person taking a stroll up and down the shoreline. Ali and Scarlotte sat on their Lilos and Greg and Darren put their towels down, creating a group circle. Drake dropped his towel next to Scarlotte and busied himself with lighting the barbecue and cooking the food.

Darren had brought a bag of beers with him which were still cold and would accompany the food perfectly.

'Hey Ali, I wonder if Nico will buy you a birthday present? Can you imagine if he buys you a ring,' Scarlotte teased her friend.

'Bloody hell, yeah, can you imagine? I have told him that I will go to the bar before I get ready for work. He said he's got me something special.'

'Oooh, exciting! Can I come with you?'

'Yes, you have to come with me so I can open it in front of you. I wonder what it is?'

'Probably a lock and key to put around your ankle so you can't leave him,' Greg said as he popped open a beer.

Nico was obsessed with Ali and she had expressed to her friends that it often felt like he was spying on her every move. He seemed to know exactly what she had been doing, where she had been and who she had been with, even before she told him.

'Wouldn't surprise me,' Ali replied as she looked around the beach feeling paranoid that Nico would be hiding behind a tree watching and listening.

'Grub's up!' Drake announced half an hour later as he got the paper plates out of the carrier bag.

'Mmm, I'm starving. It smells fantastic.' Scarlotte was first up, ready to stuff her face as always. It was amazing too - the burgers were well done on the outside and soft in the middle, the skewers were cooked to perfection and Drake had even brought along red sauce.

'Now then,' Scarlotte got everyone's attention as they hungrily took big bites of their food. 'I have a serious question to ask you all.'

'Serious, hey? What's that, Scarlotte?' Greg asked.

'OK, so here's the big question for everyone. When you have a bacon sandwich, do you have brown or red sauce on it?'

Ali sat up straight with interest, waiting for an answer

from the boys. OK, she knew she was never going to get a proper reply from this lot, but this was an important question that needed due consideration.

'Red,' replied Greg with a mouthful of food. Ali made a thumbs-up sign.

'No way, Greg - brown goes on bacon, always has and always will,' Darren said. Scarlotte punched the air.

Now the deciding vote would be in the hands of their chef for the day - Drake.

'Come on, Drake, put us out of our misery,' Ali urged.

Drake made them wait whilst he finished chewing his burger, making exaggerated noises of enjoyment.

'Mmm . . . mmm . . . *mmm*! Good chef, aren't I?' he said teasingly as they waited for his answer.

'Come *on*, Drake, stop messing about and tell us,' Ali demanded.

Silence fell. Anyone would think they were waiting for the answer to the origin of the universe or the question of whether the chicken or the egg came first. Then, suddenly:

'BROWN, OF COURSE!'

Scarlotte leapt up from her Lilo and ran around the group with her arms in the air in celebration of her win. 'Yesss, Drake! Brown *is* the best. You see, Ali?' She plonked herself back down onto her Lilo. It was as if she had just won a gold medal with her celebratory lap. So, the brown sauce versus red sauce argument was settled, although Ali was still convinced that red was best.

'Anyway, pass us the red sauce,' Scarlotte said, then squirted a large amount onto her burger which made them all laugh.

*

They had a really great afternoon on the beach eating, drinking beer and playing in the sea. Ali was loving her surprise Birthday BBQ. The boys had gone to a lot of effort to make her day special, which made both girls love their friends even more than they already did.

At half past four they rolled up their towels and put any litter in the bins by the edge of the beach.

'Are you having a good birthday?' Scarlotte asked Ali as they collected up their Lilos and towels.

'Yes, it's been the best birthday EVER.' And Ali meant it, although secretly nothing could beat having Annabel in her arms enjoying the fun with her. She was missing her little daughter badly today, but her parents had promised to phone the bar tonight and let her talk to Bel before she started work. Ali was also excited to now be heading to Cafe Marina to get her present from Nico.

The boys had gone off ahead to their apartment because Ali and Scarlotte were dawdling along, girly chatting. They took the route by Manoli's and Dimitri's shops which was the quickest way to get to Cafe Marina. Manoli was inside with some customers and waved to them as they passed. Dimitri, however, was standing with arms folded out at the front of his shop.

'Hi darling,' he said as he unfolded his arms and kissed Scarlotte on the cheek. 'How are you?'

'I'm fine, thanks - and you?' Scarlotte replied as she and Ali stood there feeling ill-at-ease and not really knowing what to say. They chatted briefly about it being Ali's birthday and what they had been up to that day. Scarlotte was thankful that Dimitri didn't ask her to go out again because now that she had spent the night with him, he no longer seemed to appeal. Scarlotte was the type of person who liked a challenge, but once that challenge was achieved, she would quickly lose interest.

'Phew.' She did a fake brow-wipe as they turned the corner into the square. 'Thank God he didn't ask me out again. I've gone off him, big-time.'

'Well, you have Spencer to take your mind off him now, don't you?' Ali replied.

When they arrived at Cafe Marina, Nico was sitting on the stool by the bar nearest to the front street.

'Happy Birthday!' He humped off his stool and ran to Ali, embracing her in a tight bearhug. Her legs left the ground as he spun her around in his arms. 'How are you, my darling? Did you celebrate your birthday on the beach?'

Ali gave Scarlotte a knowing look because it was obvious that Nico already knew exactly what she had been doing that day.

'It's been lovely, we had a barbecue.' Ali landed awkwardly after her merry-go- round ride in Nico's arms.

Nico asked Leo to make them all a cocktail to celebrate Ali's birthday. Ali had a Brandy Alexander cocktail which was her favourite, Scarlotte had an Orgasm and Nico had a Margarita.

'I have a present for you. Do you want to open it now?' Nico rushed to the back of the bar and collected a neatly wrapped little package. It definitely looked like it was going to be some sort of jewellery.

Ali clapped her hands together excitedly. 'What is it?' she asked as she started to tear off the wrapping paper.

'Open it and see, silly girl,' Nico replied. He was obviously enjoying the sight of Ali being so excited. Scarlotte leant over to see as Ali finished tearing off the paper to reveal a little blue velvet box. Slowly, she opened the box, expecting to see . . .

'Ooh, earrings! They're lovely.' Ali lifted out one of the earrings. They were long and dangly with a wooden stud, a wooden shaped feather and a real feather attached to the front. Scarlotte could see that she didn't like them and had to avert her eyes to avoid bursting out into laughter, which would have made Nico feel bad.

'Do you like them?' Nico looked mildly concerned that he had chosen the wrong gift for his love.

'Yes, they are beautiful, thank you, Nico.' Ali held them up to her ears. 'What do you think, Scarlotte?'

'Yes, they're lovely,' Scarlotte said in a choked voice. 'You should wear them tonight.' She was trying desperately not to laugh at the expression on Ali's face and took a big swig of her cocktail to disguise her grin. It went down the wrong way. Coughing and spluttering with tears of mirth, she had a valid excuse to nip off to the toilet before Nico realised that she was laughing.

Ali was wearing the earrings when Scarlotte returned. She was shaking her head from side to side to make the earrings swish about, as Nico praised her on how well they suited her. Scarlotte sat down next to her friend and shoved her straw straight in her mouth to stop the volcano of mirth which was burning inside her, ready to erupt. She couldn't make eye-contact with Ali because that would be disastrous; they'd both be in fits of laughter.

After gulping down her Orgasm, Scarlotte managed to ask Ali in a strange, squeaky voice if they were going to get ready for work. She was seriously in danger of letting it all out and needed to get away from Nico before that happened. Ali kept grinning at her, which was making matters so much worse.

Scarlotte led the way out of the bar while Ali gave Nico a kiss and a cuddle and then followed her friend down the street. Scarlotte could not yet look at Ali as they were still in full view of Nico.

'Hahaha, wait for me,' Ali giggled from behind. As soon as they turned the corner Scarlotte stopped, leant back against a wall and laughed till she cried. 'Bloody hell, Ali, that was hilarious. Your face was a picture!'

'What the hell *are* these?' Ali shook her head again, making the earrings flick about. That did it. Neither of them could speak for a good couple of minutes as they doubled over, gasping helplessly for breath.

'You have to wear them tonight though, Ali. You know that Nico will come to your bar to see you later.'

'Yeah, I know.' Ali wiped her eyes. 'Do they look stupid?'

'No, they look OK actually. You could always wear your

hair down, so they blend in with your curls. No, seriously though, Ali, they look fine. At least your present wasn't an engagement ring, so every cloud and all that!'

After pulling themselves together, and successfully managing not to wee themselves, they giggled all the way back to their apartment to get ready for the evening.

Chapter Thirty-four

'Really, Ali, the earrings look fine with your hair down.' Scarlotte was sitting on her friend's bed waiting for her to finish getting ready. Ali had taken a lot of time on her hair this evening to ensure that it was blown around the front of her neck which would then allow the earrings to blend in with her blonde curls.

'Yeah, they're not too bad, are they?' Ali shook her head from side to side, making the earrings swish about again. As it was her birthday, she had made an extra effort with her make-up and had chosen to wear her favourite white lace mini-skirt and brightly coloured floral print blouse with a ruffled cap sleeve.

'You look really lovely tonight,' Scarlotte said as she locked the apartment door behind them. 'Do you want to go out after work or are you meeting Nico?'

Ali had agreed to let Nico take her out for birthday drinks which would no doubt end up with them in his bedroom for a good birthday seeing-to. Nico lived with his parents, just as Dimitri did, which made a night of passion feel like you were a teenager sneaking around to ensure that you were not caught by your mum or dad.

'I hope Spencer comes to see you tonight.' Ali linked arms with Scarlotte as they toddled down the dusty road to work, both in their wedge sandals. 'If he does, and if you go to his place, I might ask Nico if he wants to come to our apartment. At least then I don't have to worry about making any fake pleasure noises.'

'Oh Ali, you are funny. Don't let Nico know you're faking it. You know how obsessed he is with making you happy. Just look at the gorgeous present he got you.' Scarlotte held her hands up and cupped her own ears and waltzed about the road pretending to be modelling earrings which made Ali start giggling again.

'Stop it now, you'll make my mascara run.' Ali carefully wiped the corner of her eyes with a scrunched-up tissue from her pocket.

'Hope there's no bogeys on that, you mucky bugger. Look at that tissue! And I hope it's not crispy from having been used in the bedroom with Nico.'

'Euw, stop it, Scarlotte - that's minging!' Ali stuffed the tissue back in her pocket and grinned at Scarlotte.

When they arrived at Cafe Marina, Nico had gone for a shower, so Leo was alone behind the bar. He came out, gave Ali a cuddle and wished her Happy Birthday again before making her another Brandy Alexander. Scarlotte meanwhile busied herself clearing tables and serving early bird customers who were generally couples at this time of the evening.

One young couple in particular drew her attention. They were sitting outside the bar, both facing the street. They were a good-looking pair; the guy was blond with a pretty-boy face which would not look out of place in a boy band, and the girl was petite with long brown hair tied in a ponytail. They were not talking to each other and the girl had a really bored and quite frankly pissed-off look on her face.

Scarlotte thought that they must have had a domestic because their body language was frosty, and they were leaning away from each other. She asked them if they would like another drink from the bar, but they politely declined. The guy, however, held Scarlotte's gaze a little longer than was comfortable. That was probably the reason why his girlfriend looked so unhappy, Scarlotte thought - if this was how he acted around other girls.

She had a little chat with them though and found out that they had been together for four years. They were from London and were halfway through their week's holiday. They had been out on a moped together that day to Kos

Town, and apparently the guy had been going too fast which had made the girl feel scared. She was not pleased with him at all, as she had a friend who had come off a bike in Crete and had broken her leg, resulting in huge hospital bills and a ruined holiday. She was scared that the same would happen to her.

As soon as Scarlotte left them alone, they stopped talking again and sat there looking away from each other.

'I reckon they've had a fall-out,' Scarlotte whispered to Ali who was still sitting at the bar. She was now using the scabby tissue to wipe off a dribble of cocktail from the front of her blouse.

'Bloody hell, Ali, let me get you a clean tissue.' She took the vile tissue off Ali, being careful to only touch it with her forefinger and thumb, pinched her nose and dropped it into the bin behind the bar. 'Here.' She handed her one of the clean serviettes which were used for customers who ordered toasties - the only food they served in the Café Marina.

'He's a bit of a dish, isn't he?' Ali's eyes flicked over to the couple outside. 'He keeps looking at you, Scarlotte. Shame he's with his girlfriend - I reckon you'd be in there.'

As Scarlotte looked over to the couple, the guy caught her eye and gave her a smile.

Ali said, 'Told you so,' then got up to announce that she was leaving for work. At the same time the couple got up and walked off in the opposite direction to Ali. Scarlotte stood at the front of the bar and waved her friend off and then glanced over at the couple. The guy turned around and locked eyes with Scarlotte, which made her feel kind of tingly inside. He was indeed a complete dish.

The first thing Nico asked Scarlotte when he arrived at the bar was whether Ali liked her earrings. He had sensed that she found them amusing rather than beautiful, which was what he had hoped for. Scarlotte reassured him that Ali did indeed like his gift, and that she often looked amused when she was happy - so he was not to worry. Besides, Ali was wearing them tonight which was a good sign that she liked them. Feeling better now, Nico's expression instantly changed from one of concern to the wide grin of a Cheshire cat.

By midnight, Spencer still hadn't come into the bar and Scarlotte had resigned herself to the fact that he wasn't going to turn up. He had obviously taken her absence last night as a sign of her lack of interest in him. Absurd, she thought. How could he think that any girl would not be interested in him? She would just have to go to his beach to explain her absence.

She was serving the last group of customers outside when the blond London guy from earlier pulled up on a moped and parked it next to the bar. He said hello to Scarlotte and went inside, sat at the bar and ordered a bottle of Amstel beer.

'Didn't expect to see you back,' Scarlotte said as she walked by him with a handful of empty glasses and carefully placed them in the sink.

'I needed to get out for a while,' he said and took a big swig of his beer. Scarlotte pulled up a stool next to him and discovered that his name was Ollie and that he and his girlfriend had had a huge row earlier that day over the moped episode. She still wasn't talking to him and her bad mood was ruining their holiday. He wasn't sure, in fact, if he still wanted her as his girlfriend. Ollie and Scarlotte chatted easily together as she carried on cleaning up the last of the customers' tables.

At the end of the evening, Ollie was still sitting at the bar as Scarlotte and Nico brought in the tables and chairs from out the front.

'Want a lift home?' Ollie asked as Nico got the keys ready to lock up.

'OK - thanks. But don't be riding too fast now though,' she cautioned, and bumped into his shoulder, knocking him off-balance.

Ollie mounted the moped, started it up and turned it around ready for Scarlotte to get on the back. She climbed on and pressed the inside of her thighs tightly around Ollie's legs. She then wrapped her arms around his waist and could feel his toned abs beneath his white T-shirt. He shuffled back a bit, pressing his bum into her groin area which felt nice, really *really* nice, in fact. She could smell his freshly washed hair as she leant forward and put her chin on his left shoulder. If this guy were single, he would definitely be boyfriend material.

The ride to Scarlotte's apartment was literally only five minutes away, so their journey would be very short. 'Fancy sitting on the beach for a bit?' Ollie shouted over the sound of the moped.

'OK, why not. Turn left here and there's a little beach at the end of the resort.' Scarlotte directed Ollie to another quiet area of the beach; at this time of the night every beach was quiet anyway.

As they parked up and dismounted, Ollie opened the seat of the moped and produced a couple of beers. 'I've come prepared.' He displayed the beers, winked and gave Scarlotte a triumphant grin.

After passing her a beer, they sat on sunbeds next to each other.

'The stars are so bright here,' Scarlotte said dreamily. She loved anything to do with space, planets and science.

'Yeah, they look beautiful - just like you.'

'Don't let your girlfriend hear you say that.' She really liked this guy; he was kind of sweet and she felt as if she had known him a long time.

'I have an idea. Fancy going skinny dipping?' Ollie looked over at Scarlotte, waiting for an answer.

'Come on then.' Scarlotte looked around to check that there was no one else close by. It was pitch black though as there were no lights on this part of the beach, so even if there were people around, they would need to have their night-vision goggles on to be able spot them. Ollie whipped off his jeans, T-shirt and boxer shorts and dived into the sea. Scarlotte put her clothes neatly on the sunbed and tiptoed naked into the calm night sea.

'Jesus, it's cold!' She had her arms wrapped around her front, in an attempt to keep her boobs warm. Ollie swam towards her and splashed her naked body, making her scream before swimming off again.

Once fully submerged in the freezing-cold water, Scarlotte swam over to Ollie who was standing on his tiptoes to keep his head above the water. He instinctively put his arms around her waist and pulled her towards him. She wrapped her legs around his naked body and could feel his hardness pressing against her. It felt so wrong being in the night sea with Ollie because he had a girlfriend, but at the same time it was so exhilarating and felt so right.

'You are so beautiful,' he murmured before engaging her in a passionate kiss to which she fully responded. They made love in the sea and it was the most exciting lovemaking that Scarlotte had experienced since arriving on the island. And it was made even more special by the fact that this was an unexpected and wonderful encounter. It was also a bit risky without condoms, but Scarlotte knew her period was about to come on, so it should be safe. Also, Ollie and his girlfriend had been in a relationship for four years, so she needn't fear catching the dreaded STD.

They took big strides out of the sea and walked hand-in-hand to their sunbeds. The night air was warm but they both felt cold from the chilly seawater. Ollie had a small towel packed in the seat of the moped and he handed it to Scarlotte to dry herself. Once half dry, she gave it back to Ollie, who was sitting shivering on his sunbed. She quickly dressed and squeezed herself next to him to warm up. He wrapped his arms around her, and they lay in silence, warm again and gazing up at the sky.

'Look!' Scarlotte pointed as a shooting star swished over their heads.

'Wow! And there's another!' Ollie said excitedly.

They lay in each other's arms for a good hour trying to spot more shooting stars before they decided that Ollie should really go back to his hotel, and to his girlfriend. They climbed onto the moped and Scarlotte directed him to her apartment.

'Thanks for a lovely night,' she said as she climbed off the back. Ollie remained on the moped and pulled her towards him for one last passionate kiss before spinning the bike around and zooming off into the night. 'Good night, gorgeous!' he shouted.

Chapter Thirty-five

Scarlotte got inside the flat and could hear laughter coming from Ali's bedroom. She smiled to herself as she heard Nico tell Ali to put the earrings back on. She was probably naked, and he wanted her to just be wearing his birthday gift whilst they made love.

She crept into her own bedroom, closed the door and stripped off her damp clothes.

Her mouth felt really dry, so she took a sip from the bottle of water on her bedside table and screwed up her face at the salty taste on her lips. The water was warm from being left out of the fridge, but that was exactly as Scarlotte liked it - cold water just hurt her sensitive teeth. She had really enjoyed her night on the beach with Ollie but knew that she probably wouldn't see him again. She also couldn't wait for the morning so she could tell Ali all about it.

Scarlotte was up early in the morning. She was desperate for a warm shower and also wanted to go into the square first thing to call her mum. They hadn't spoken for a few days now, so it was time for a catch-up. She really should write a letter or call Lisa at some point as she had so much to tell her. Passing Ali's room with the door now wide open, she could see that Nico had gone and Ali was fast asleep on top of the bed with her sheet just about covering up her lady bits. Scarlotte had a quick coffee and a fag on the balcony, left Ali a note and popped out to the shops to get a phonecard.

'Hello, darling daughter, how are you?' Eve sounded in good spirits as always. She had been out with her boyfriend Steve last night for a meal at her favourite Italian restaurant. Scarlotte could guess what she'd eaten: her mum always had Steak Diane and garlic bread, her favourite items on the menu.

Scarlotte filled her mum in on the week's antics with Spencer who had collected her in the speedboat, his parachute drop, and how their gang had had a great time on the beach for Ali's birthday. Eve asked her to pass on birthday wishes to Ali from her. Scarlotte wouldn't tell her mum all of the details of the last week, and certainly not about skinny-dipping in the sea with someone else's boyfriend, because they didn't really talk about that type of thing. Eve said she was missing her, but that she would have Scarlotte back at home for the winter at least. The phone card lasted just long enough for them both to say their goodbyes, and to send each other kisses and their love.

Scarlotte always had mixed feelings after she had spoken with her mum. She missed her dearly, which made her heart ache - but she was having the time of her life in Kos. After the phone call, she popped into the bakery in the square and picked up two sweet pastries and take-away coffees for herself and Ali. The smell of the bakery was so good first thing in the morning and it was no surprise that it was always busy. As she walked out of the door with her hands full, she bumped into Dimitri and almost spilt the coffees.

'Oops – sorry, darling. How are you?' Dimitri was also getting his morning coffee fix from the bakery before opening his shop.

'I'm fine, thanks. How are you?' Scarlotte fiddled with coffee cups, pushing the plastics lids on tight again as she held the pastry bag between her teeth.

Dimitri said he too was fine and asked Scarlotte if she fancied going out again that night.

'Oh thanks, but I can't tonight. I've made plans with Ali,' Scarlotte lied as there was no way she would be going out with him again, especially with so many other hunks to choose from. She promised she would go and see him in his shop at some point, but she knew that she definitely would not.

After escaping the excruciating encounter with Dimitri, Scarlotte walked briskly back to the apartment to eat her pastry and drink her coffee with Ali before they went cold.

Ali was sitting on their balcony smoking a fag with just a beach towel wrapped around her body and one earring in.

'Morning, lovely. Are you hungry?' Scarlotte put the pastries and coffee on the table in front of Ali.

'Ooh yes, you are a star! How's your mum?' Ali put out her cigarette, ripped open the brown paper bag containing the pastries, and hungrily took one out and began to eat it.

'She's doing good, thanks. She said to wish you a Happy Birthday for yesterday. How was your evening with Nico? I can see that you're still wearing *one* of your earrings.'

Ali put her hands up to her ears. 'Oh God, the other will probably be somewhere in the bed, or stuck to Nico's bum,' which made them both giggle. 'I'll look for it later. Anyway, did Spencer come to see you?'

Ali sat with her mouth wide open with her pastry going cold in her hand as Scarlotte told her that she had not seen Spencer but that she had been skinny-dipping with Ollie.

'Bloody hell, mate - and his girlfriend was back at their hotel? It's a good job she didn't come looking for him. She sounds like a miserable cow anyway.' Ali tutted and wiped the sugar from her mouth with the corner of her towel. 'Do you want to go to Spencer's beach today?'

'Do you know what? I can't be bothered. If he's interested, he'll just have to come looking for me.'

'Good girl. It's his loss if he doesn't, and let's face it, you're not short of offers by the sound of things. Hey, I had to tell Nico about Annabel last night. He saw her photo on my bedside table. He was really sweet about it and said that he can't wait to meet her.'

'Oh Ali, that's great news. He could be her new daddy after all' Scarlotte winked at Ali who was rolling her eyes at the thought.

They sat enjoying their breakfast in the morning

sunshine telling each other details of their evenings. They talked about Nico, Ollie, Spencer and Dimitri, and how Scarlotte never fancied anyone after she had finally shagged them. It was true though; the excitement of the chase had gone, and she would always look for the next challenge.

Chapter Thirty-six

Ali found her second earring covered in fluff. It had fallen on the floor behind the bed. She batted off the fluff and put both earrings in their little box for safekeeping and tucked them into the front pocket of her grey suitcase. She would leave them there for now – well, for the remainder of their time in Kos, as she did feel rather silly wearing them. Today, she was really missing her daughter back at home and momentarily felt a little bit teary. She'd never been away for so long before but had called home religiously every other day to check on her little girl. Her parents were taking good care of Bel and were taking her out on day trips and generally ensuring that she had fun whilst Ali was away.

Although Ali was loving her time in Kos, the thought of throwing her arms around her precious baby girl was drawing her back to England.

'Are you OK? You're a bit quiet this morning.' The girls were at the usual beach and Scarlotte had noticed that Ali was a little subdued, quite unlike her usual bouncy self.

'I'm OK, thanks, but I'm just looking forward to having a cuddle with my daughter,' Ali mumbled. She was face down, topless on her sunbed absorbing the morning sunshine.

'Ah, bless you, it won't be long now before you see her. Actually, we really should go to the travel agents and book our flight back before they sell out. I think the last flight is the second of November. We might need to fly to Athens first and then back home from there.' Their time in Kos was now limited, which gave them both mixed feelings. Thinking of home, Scarlotte realised that she still hadn't called Lisa. They would definitely be in need of a massive catch up when she got back now.

'Stick us a bit of baby oil on my back, will you.' Ali passed Scarlotte the bottle from under her sunbed.

'Jesus, Ali, it's covered in sand! Did you want an exfoliation treatment?'

'Don't rub my tan off, will you.'

Scarlotte carefully dripped the oil onto Ali's back, trying not to let any sand fall off the bottle onto her skin.

'Put some on yourself,' Ali said 'You'll get a darker tan.'

'Don't you think I'll burn?' Scarlotte herself used oil but it was generally at least a factor 4.

'No, you'll be fine. Your skin should be used to the sun by now.' Ali relaxed as Scarlotte gently rubbed the oil into her back.

'Wahey! What exactly is going on here? Can I watch?' Greg jumped off the wall sending a sandstorm in their direction.

'Bloody hell, Greg,' Scarlotte said crossly and tried to brush the sand off Ali's back.

'You're such a perve, Greg,' Ali mumbled. 'You're only jealous because she's not putting oil on *your* back.' Ali wasn't wrong: Greg would have loved Scarlotte to be applying oil onto his back, and no doubt on other parts of his body too.

'Hey, girls, look at these pictures.' Greg pulled a little digital camera out of his pocket. He had bought it from the same shop that produced the workers' party photos. It was the latest in modern technology and you could actually see your photos before you had them printed off.

'Oh wow, that looks cool. Let's have a look.' Scarlotte held out her oily hand to Greg.

'Oi, get your greasy mitts off. You look with your eyes, not with your hands.' Greg held his own hand over the screen to shade the sunshine, allowing Scarlotte to look at his pictures.

'What the hell?' Scarlotte was shocked as Greg showed her photos of a naked woman sprawled out on his bed.

'Gorgeous, isn't she?' He flicked through the shots of the woman who was obviously happy to have her lady bits on display for the camera.

'Let's have a look.' Ali sat up, making her boobs wobble about before covering them with her T-shirt. 'Oh my God, who is she?' Ali's eyes were popping out of her head as she looked at the rude pictures of Greg's latest conquest.

'Suzanne, she's on holiday with her sister. She's been flirting with me all week and last night I finally scored. She goes home today though.'

Greg went on to tell them how Suzanne, a young woman of about twenty-five years old, had been coming on to him all week. She had been going to his bar every night with her sister and apart from last night, he hadn't seen her after the sisters left his bar to get a meal. Last night was different though. Suzanne had gone back to the bar just as Greg was clearing up and she had snogged his face off in the middle of the street. Greg had taken her back to his apartment for a 'right good rogering' as he called it. He had been showing her his new toy (and his camera), and she had willingly posed for him to take some naked shots of her.

'I bet she didn't think you were going to show the whole town the pictures though, eh, did she?' And Ali slapped Greg's knee.

'She'll be on her flight home now, so no one will see her again.' Greg didn't hold any emotional attachment to the women he shagged, it was just a bit of fun for him. He was enjoying the single life too much to let any woman get under his skin.

Scarlotte started to apply the baby oil onto her legs which made them look lovely and glossy and brown.

'What the fuck are you doing? You'll burn like hell with that stuff on.' Greg stared at Scarlotte's long legs as she applied the oil right up to the top of her thighs.

'I'll be all right. Ali uses it all of the time.'

'Yes, but Ali has darker skin than you, you idiot. Don't

say I didn't warn you.'

Ignoring his warning, Scarlotte continued to apply the baby oil all over her body, including her face, before pushing Greg's bum off her sunbed and making herself comfortable.

Greg pulled up a sunbed next to Scarlotte. 'Do my back, darlin',' he wheedled.

'Bloody hell, Greg, I've just got comfy.' Scarlotte sat up again and rubbed Greg's own orange carrot oil into his back. 'Do you two think I'm your personal masseuse? I hope you realise that I will be waking you both up later to do my back for me.' She finished applying the oil to Greg's back before laying herself back down to fry in the sun.

'Where are Darren and Drake today?' Ali asked Greg as she also made herself more comfortable face-down on her sunbed.

Apparently, they hadn't gone back to their apartment last night, so Greg said that they must have 'pulled' and had stopped over at their respective conquests' apartments.

'You boys are so naughty,' Scarlotte tutted, and then realised that she was actually being a little bit hypocritical considering her skinny-dipping episode with a complete stranger last night.

The three of them soon nodded off in the sunshine. They were all knackered from their late nights and nothing would wake them for a good couple of hours.

*

'JESUS! Wake up, Scarlotte.' Drake and Darren had arrived at the beach and woke them all from their snooze.

'What's up?' Scarlotte sat up sleepily.

'Look at the state of your face! You look like a lobster!' Drake was doing an impression of lobster claws with his hands and nipping Scarlotte's leg. 'You're going to need some cream on that later, dearie.'

'I've got some special cream that will help,' Greg said crudely, pointing at his groin area. Then, as he looked at

Scarlotte's bright red face, he added, 'I did tell you not to put that oil on.'

'Is it really bad?' She held up her hands to her hot red face.

'We'll have to get you some natural yoghurt on the way back. It's really good for sunburn.' Ali was feeling bad for letting Scarlotte use her baby oil. The guys, however, thought it was highly amusing and would of course take the piss out of Scarlotte for the remainder of the day.

*

'Ouch ouch ouch *ouch*!' The shower was burning the front of Scarlotte's body.

'What on earth are you doing in there!' Ali shouted from outside the bathroom door.

'It's just that the shower feels like it's melting my sunburnt skin.' Scarlotte climbed out of the shower and inspected her body in the full-length bathroom mirror. 'Jesus Christ, I look like a tube of striped toothpaste.' Her skin was bright red at the front in contrast to the paler skin on her back.

Ali was waiting outside the bathroom door. They had purchased some yoghurt on the way back from the beach but there was no way that Scarlotte could go to work smelling like a gone-off bottle of milk. She applied some normal after-sun which helped a little to soothe her lobster-coloured skin and stepped outside the bathroom.

'Poor you.' Ali held her hands up to her mouth as she inspected her friend's sunburn. 'I feel really guilty for telling you to put that baby oil on. Are you all right?'

'Yeah, I'm fine. I'm sure it will go down by tomorrow.' Scarlotte wasn't so sure that it would, but she didn't want Ali to feel bad. Anyway, she herself had chosen to put it on: it wasn't as though Ali had twisted her arm up her back to make her apply it.

After painfully pulling on her skinny jeans to hide her bright red legs, Scarlotte looked for a suitable top to wear which wouldn't clash with her Rudolph the Red-Nosed Reindeer schnozzle. The red top was *definitely* out of the question and white would just make her look like a matchstick - the black one would be the best option. She applied some pressed powder to her face in an attempt to tone down her shiny red fizzog.

'Do I look really dreadful?' She went into Ali's room and stood with her arms outside at shoulder height to display her exposed areas of skin.

'No, mate, honestly you look fine now that you've put some make-up on. Your arms look sore though. Do you feel all right? You don't feel shivery or headachy, do you?'

'No, I'm fine. Why do you ask? Do I look pale?' Scarlotte replied, making them both laugh.

'You definitely don't look pale, but make sure you don't drink alcohol but do drink lots of water tonight, won't you. I don't want you fainting from sunstroke.' It was good advice from Ali as alcohol would just make her super-dehydrated.

*

Work that night for Scarlotte would be a painful affair on two accounts. Firstly, she would have to deal with Nico and Leo taking the piss out of her for the whole evening, and secondly, she did start to feel shivery despite only drinking water. On the advice of Ali, she had taken a little cardigan to wear just in case she did start to feel ill, and halfway through her shift she put the cardigan on. She was serving drinks and collecting glasses in what looked like winter attire. If she had a drachma for every time someone asked the question, 'Aren't you hot in that cardigan?' she would have been a very wealthy lady.

The evening dragged and all she wanted to do was go back to the apartment, have a cold shower and get into bed. A group of guys from her hometown Nottingham had come in for a drink. They were on holiday for a week and had just arrived the previous night. One of them, Andrew, worked at a car dealership just around the corner from her mum's house. Scarlotte knew it well as it was the garage where she had tried to sell her jeep, earlier that year. She promised to pop in and see him when she was home for the winter. Andrew was a sweet guy but not really her type. He would make a good friend, she thought.

The guys didn't stay for long in the bar, only for one drink, as they needed to explore the rest of the nightlife. They asked Leo to take a photo of them together with Scarlotte before she waved them off, again promising to go and see Andrew when she arrived back in the UK.

By eleven o'clock Scarlotte was starting to feel quite poorly, but the bar was really busy tonight and there was no way that she would be able to leave early. Drinking so much water was also making her go for a wee every half an hour which was annoying, and she didn't want Nico to think that she was just skiving off for a break. She soldiered on, placing a warm welcoming smile on her face as always – and her cheeks and forehead were now greasy as well as bright red.

She was just making an Irish coffee in the back for a customer and licking the delicious cream off the spoon when she heard Spencer's voice coming from the bar. He would have to come in today, wouldn't he, when she was looking like a twat with her red face.

'Hi, gorgeous.' Spencer looked as delicious as always and was sitting at the end of the bar with a beer.

'Hi! Let me serve this coffee and I'll be back.' Scarlotte swiftly served the drink to the customer and headed back inside to talk to her hunky surfer dude.

'Can't believe you stood me up the other night. I spent ages waiting for you.' Spencer was smiling as he spoke, so she could see that he wasn't annoyed.

'I literally walked the streets trying to find your door. Are you sure it's yellow? You're not colour blind, are you?' Scarlotte enquired.

'Yes, it is yellow, cheeky, and it's just two streets down. Do I need to draw you a map?'

Scarlotte picked up a white paper serviette and found a pen next to the till. Spencer drew a simple map of directions with himself as a stick man at the door and handed the serviette back to Scarlotte.

'Ooh, looks just like you,' Scarlotte grinned, pointing at the stick man.

'Are you coming over tonight? I'll put a note on the door, so you know you've got the right place.' Spencer looked expectantly at Scarlotte. It was funny how the sight of him suddenly made her feel much better.

'Yes, OK, but I'm feeling a bit off today, so I probably won't stay long.'

'OK, gorgeous, that's fine. I'll wait up for you.' Spencer downed the last of his beer and placed the bottle on the bar before kissing Scarlotte on the cheek and saying he'd see her later.

It was 1.30 a.m. before the last customers left the bar. Nico and Leo would shut the bar that evening, Nico said, and would let Scarlotte go home, as he could see that she was not feeling too well.

After leaving the bar, Scarlotte pulled the serviette out of her pocket. Right, this can't be too difficult, she thought as she turned the map the right way up.

Surprisingly, Spencer's place was exactly where she had been walking the other night. The door was white with just a hint of yellow, so it was no wonder that she had missed it. Spencer had placed a notice on the door with a big arrow pointing upwards and the words THIS DOOR. Scarlotte slowly opened the door and peered inside. There were steps leading up to three more doors. Spencer had also put a note on his door which read COME IN with another stick man underneath the words. She felt a little nervous just walking into the apartment. What if she'd got it wrong and the note was left by someone else? 'Don't be fucking stupid,' she said to herself. It would be a major coincidence if someone else had put these notes up.

She opened the metal-framed door, crept inside and carefully closed the door behind her, trying *really* hard not to make too much noise as it clicked shut. The apartment was small, in fact it was more like a hotel room than an apartment. The bedroom was actually the main room with a door to the left which must have been the bathroom.

At first, she couldn't see Spencer. She whispered, 'Hello, hello, hello,' before realising that he was tucked up under his covers fast asleep. Thoughts of him waking and thinking that she was an intruder ran through her mind. What if he was startled and tried to wrestle her to the floor - which she wouldn't have minded, to be honest. She stood there for a minute wondering whether she should disturb him. He looked as if he was in a deep sleep and it seemed unfair to wake him up.

As she was now again feeling a bit crap, she decided to quietly tiptoe back out of the apartment and go home to her own bed. At least she now knew where he lived, and she could come over tomorrow night instead.

The evening breeze felt refreshing on Scarlotte's poor burnt face as she headed back up to the hill to the apartment. When safely inside she popped her head around Ali's door to see her fast asleep inside her bedcovers tonight. After taking the yoghurt from the fridge, Scarlotte stripped off her clothes and lay on top of her bed; she couldn't be arsed to have a shower, nor to slather herself in the yoghurt. She fell asleep almost instantly, leaving the yoghurt on the side table to grow its own penicillin overnight.

Chapter Thirty-seven

'That's eighty drachmas each, please.' The girl in the travel agents had managed to get them on the last flight from Kos to Birmingham airport. They would have to fly to Athens first and get a connecting flight from there. Fortunately, they had both saved just enough money to pay for the flights and reluctantly handed over their crumpled notes.

'I don't want to leave,' Scarlotte said as they left the shop, pulling her bottom lip down to make a silly sad face. Their adventure was coming to an end and her heart felt really heavy. They would have just one week left in Kos so they must make the most of it. Linking arms, they went for a Full English, with chips of course, which always cheered them up.

Darren and Drake were also treating themselves to a FEB when they arrived at the restaurant by their beach. Greg was sitting on the beach reading his crappy newspaper as usual.

'We've just booked our flights home,' Scarlotte said solemnly with eyes cast down as she fiddled with the salt pot on the table.

'We booked ours yesterday too. We fly home in two days,' Drake mumbled through a mouthful of toast.

The boys had managed to get a direct flight back to Cardiff which was their closest airport to home. Greg had also booked his flight back to Liverpool on the same day.

'Oh no! Does that include today or two days after today?' Scarlotte asked.

'Two more days after today, so we have today and tomorrow left on the beach, because we'll need to pack the day after for our flight,' Darren said, also looking a bit down in the mouth.

As they all ate in relative silence, which was most

unusual for them, Scarlotte's mind was cast back to the things that she had done during her season in Kos. She really had had the best time and would remember this experience for the rest of her life.

*

The gang's last couple of days went far too quickly. They spent time together on the beach during the day and worked at their respective bars and restaurants at night. When it came time for the boys to fly home, Scarlotte and Ali went to the airport with them. After swapping home phone numbers and addresses, they bade each other a heart-wrenching farewell. The girls left the airport in tears after waving the boys off as they went through security. Scarlotte had not seen Spencer again - he had probably given up hope of her turning up after being let down twice now. Ali was still dating Nico and he'd promised to visit her in England during the winter.

Scarlotte and Ali felt a bit lost without the boys being around. On their last day they had a drink with the guys from the watersports. Ali had given them all a last haircut on the beach before they too left the island for the winter season.

Nico took them to the airport on their last day, and as they walked together towards the departures area Scarlotte tripped with her rucksack on her back and fell onto the hard, gravelly ground. She was literally pinned there by her heavy rucksack and was wriggling about like a beached whale trying desperately to get back into the sea.

'Oh my God, what happened?' Ali knelt down and tried to help her friend up off the floor, while Nico grabbed her rucksack and lifted it up from the back with Scarlotte's body still attached and dangling like a ragdoll from the front.

'Bloody hell, look at my knee!' Scarlotte batted the gravel off her hands and looked at the blood streaming down her left knee into her shin.

'Here, take my tissue.' Ali pulled out one of her crumpled tissues from her jeans pocket and tried to hand it to Scarlotte.

'No thanks, mate,' came the reply. 'I think I'll let it bleed.'

Epilogue

A Saturday afternoon in May

The wasp had buzzed off by now, and Scarlotte pulled her mind back to the present day.

She'd been reliving her time in Kos for the last couple of hours whilst dozing on and off on her sunbed. It had all felt so real, as if she had truly been back there. Sometimes, reality and dreams blended into one and you were not quite sure which bits were real and which were figments of your imagination.

'Want a glass of wine?' Eve called from the kitchen window.

'Oooh, yes please, Mum.' Scarlotte sat up and adjusted the back of her sunbed into a suitable drinking position, ready for wine o'clock.

The Sauvignon Blanc was lovely and chilled. Eve had filled the glasses to the brim as she always did, which would avoid having to make unnecessary trips back to the fridge.

'You've had a lovely lazy afternoon, haven't you?' her mum said tenderly. 'You've been miles away, ducky, haven't you?'

'Yes, Mum,' Scarlotte said, and felt a happy-sad tear trickle unseen down her cheek. 'I was just reminiscing.'

If you enjoyed this novel, make sure to read the next in the series:

Scarlotte's Memoirs
Back for More - Season 2 in Kos

Chapter One

Winter, 1993

Scarlotte Henson had been back in her home town of Nottingham for just a week now after returning from working on the Greek island of Kos for the entire summer season. She had had the most amazing adventures in the resort of Kardamena with her new friend Ali, whom she had met on a flight to the island earlier that year. The two girls had hit it off immediately and become the best of friends, sharing so many adventures of all kinds. They told each other everything – whether it was good news, bad news, romantic, sexual or often plain embarrassing!

Whatever it was, they would end up laughing fit to burst.

But now it was back to reality. Scarlotte knew it was going to be a long, cold English winter before she could return to Kos next May for another season of working in Café Marina. She missed Ali, who was miles away in Birmingham. In the meantime, she knew she would have to find a normal job, so she could save up to go back for a second season in Kos.

*

'I need you to do a typing test for me,' said the snooty girl in the recruitment agency.

No problem. Scarlotte could type fast and blasted through the test in record time. Suitably impressed with her secretarial skills, the agency phoned her at home the same afternoon to offer her a temporary position in an NHS office. The best thing was that the office was literally a ten-minute walk from her mum's house. She was booked to start the following morning at 8.30 a.m.

On hearing the news, Scarlotte dashed upstairs and went through her wardrobe, chucking everything aside as she looked for respectable office-type clothes. God knows what she was going to wear as most of her skimpy outfits were now only suitable for the hot climate of Greece. There, jeans or a bikini, a long-sleeved T-shirt tied around her waist and a pair of flipflops were her normal attire. But now, even her tan was already beginning to fade.

'Can I borrow your black polo-neck jumper, Mum?' she called downstairs, where Eve was doing the ironing. 'I've literally got nothing to wear.'

'Yes, of course,' Eve called back. 'It's in the left-hand side of my wardrobe.'

Scarlotte then dug around in her own chest of drawers and eventually found a mustard-coloured, knee-length woollen skirt, a pair of thick black tights and black ankle boots to complete her office attire.

The next morning, wearing her big coat and scarf, she made her way out into the chilly November morning to go and start her new temporary job. She was feeling a bit down and depressed, her head and heart still full of Greece and wishing she could be back with her friends.

However, unbeknownst to her at that time, the next few months would be full of surprises, bringing more adventures, more laughter, and of course more boys . . . enough to keep Scarlotte's hands and heart full until at last she went back to Kos for another season of non-stop, full-on life under the hot Greek sun.

read on . . .

Printed in Great Britain
by Amazon

50145005R00127